LOUIS L'AMOUR

THE RIDERS
OF
HIGH ROCK

A HOPALONG CASSIDY NOVEL

BANTAM BOOKS
NEW YORK · TORONTO · LONDON · SYDNEY · AUCKLAND

THE RIDERS OF HIGH ROCK

A Bantam Book

Bantam Hardcover / June 1993
The Louis L'Amour Collection / June 1993

Previously published as *Hopalong Cassidy and the Riders of High Rock*
by Louis L'Amour (writing as Tex Burns).

ISBN 0-553-06324-3

Published simultaneously in the United States and Canada

Bantam Books are published by Bantam Books, a division of Bantam
Doubleday Dell Publishing Group, Inc. Its trademark, consisting of the
words "Bantam Books" and the portrayal of a rooster, is Registered in
U.S. Patent and Trademark Office and in other countries. Marca
Registrada. Bantam Books, 1540 Broadway, New York, New York 10036.

PRINTED IN THE UNITED STATES OF AMERICA

KPH 0 9 8 7 6 5 4 3 2 1

THE RIDERS
OF
HIGH ROCK

A HOPALONG CASSIDY NOVEL

CHAPTER 1

Chase in the Mountains

As Red Connors put the sorrel up the slope he felt the big horse break stride and knew that it was all in. From the top of the hill Red could see the cloud of dust marking pursuit, but realized that he was out of sight, for the time being at least. Grimly he stared at the rifle in the saddle scabbard. If he just had some more cartridges!

This Winchester in the hands of Red Connors had done phenomenal shooting, but now he had no more ammunition and even his six-shooter was empty. There was a bloody wound in his side and unless he quickly found somewhere to hide he was a gone gosling.

More than once in these past few days he had thought of his old friend Hopalong Cassidy. There was no one like him for planning a way out or around, and no one like him with a six-gun either. Right then Red Connors would have given almost anything if he could have seen Hopalong come over the rise ahead of him.

He turned the sorrel along the ridge, keeping to the broken country and putting as many pines between himself and the direction of the pursuit as possible. He knew this was a race with death, and the men behind him had every intention of leaving him for the buzzards.

Yet it was not his own life alone that hung in the balance, but the lives and hopes of his friends on the 3TL. With what he now knew, there was every chance they might finally end the systematic cattle stealing that he suspected had been going on in the High Rock country for the last several months. However, that was the very reason the rustlers could not let him live.

Before him the mountain broke off sharply, offering a magnificent view of the sunken gorges and the distant Sawtooth Range far to the north. The path he had followed was an ancient game trail; now he turned off it, holding to a rocky shelf to leave no prints, and headed down-slope into a grove of aspen and mountain laurel. Far below he could see the brilliant blue of a small lake, set like a jewel among the towering peaks and the ranges about it.

The sorrel plodded wearily, and Red knew that behind him his enemies would be gaining. Their own animals were fresh. Sooner or later they would corner him.

Sweat trickled down Red's face and he removed his hat, wiping his hand over his sparse red hair. Suddenly he saw a steep footpath, turning down the face of the cliff to the right of the trail, and instantly he decided to gamble. Swinging down, he hastily stripped his saddle and bridle from the exhausted horse and, hitting it a thump on the shoulder, swung towards the trail.

He staggered now, almost dropping the heavy saddle. Fifty feet down the steep path he found a tiny ledge, a place that offered a little shelter from above, and into which no man could gain entry as long as Red remained conscious and able to resist, for the narrowness of the path was such that it would be very easy to overbalance an attacker and send him crashing down the face of the cliff.

Above him he heard horses, then voices. The riders reined in and he heard them talking. "Aw! Don't tell me that! I hit the redheaded billy goat, and you know it! No use to chase him! He's done for!"

"Here's his trail," a new voice said. "His horse broke stride here, but kept on goin'. He won't get far now, and it's a long ways until dark. We got him wherever he is."

"Mount up, then," a third voice said. "Hoyt, you and Mex stay here until we send up a smoke or signal you. He might try to double back over the mountain."

"No chance. That redhead's done for!" The speaker cleared his throat. "And I'm just as glad! He could shoot!"

There was a sound of horses moving off and then silence. A boot scuffed on rock and then a match scratched. "Me, I'm pleased to be here," a voice said. "I've had enough of ridin' for one week. That hombre was sure hard to catch!"

"Señor, 'ave you see thees trail? She's been travel' recent!"

Red Connors stiffened. Half dead with exhaustion as he was, he forced his muscles to alertness and waited, tense with effort.

Now Hoyt scoffed. "Ain't been nobody down there but a goat! And if there was," he added, "you want to go down that trail after him? I don't!"

Red Connors backed up and sat down. For the first time he had a chance to examine his wound. The slug had cut through the flesh of his side, but although his clothing was soaked with blood, the wound didn't look serious. He looked again at his canteen. It was empty. They had given him no time to stop and refill. Like cowhands cutting a steer, they had kept after him, keeping him away from water, away from town, away from main trails. Whichever way he headed they were ready for him and had turned him back.

Worse, they seemed to know how much ammunition he had. They had drawn him into a fire fight, they had given him chances, and he knew he had killed two horses and crippled at least one man. But that was only after he had learned that what ammunition he had was in his belt. His rifle and pistol had been empty—and that meant somebody had made sure they were empty, for he never left them so. Somebody on the 3TL was a traitor; somebody there wanted him dead.

Sagging back against the wall, he fought for consciousness. Pain mounted through his exhausted body and waves of darkness went over him. Over the mountains the sun was bright and hot. The slow afternoon drew on, the coolness and darkness came, and Red Connors lay sprawled full length in the tiny hollow of rock where he had fallen.

Twelve miles to the south Hopalong Cassidy rode along the main trail towards the cow town of Tascotal and the 3TL Ranch. Hopalong had been in the saddle all day and he was tired. The trail was good and the excellent steeldust gelding he rode was a horse that liked to travel. He had left Topper on the other side of the mountain, suffering from a temporary lameness. Hopalong had hired a man to bring him out to Gibson's when Topper recovered.

Farther south, long chains of mountains stretched away from the trail, and to the north, beyond the foothills were towering ranges, all clad with pines and firs, some capped with crowns of snow. The wheel marks of the stage were in the road, but there were few other signs of passing until he reached White Rock Wells.

Filling his canteen at the Wells, he looked around from long habit and saw signs left by a body of at least six riders. All had been armed and ready, for he saw the marks left by the rifle stocks in the damp sand. They had been leaned against a rock while their owners drank. Men carrying rifles in their hands usually meant trouble . . . so it might pay to ride carefully on the way into town.

Several of the men had smoked cigarettes here, and there had been a fire where they made coffee. Then four horses had ridden on and two had remained at the spring. Where were those two now?

His ears caught a whisper of sound and he wheeled just in time to see two men emerge from the woods. They were staring, wild-eyed, and even as their eyes met, both men grabbed for their guns.

Then their hands froze, for they were looking into the muzzles of a pair of Colt .45's. Hopalong's flashing, lightning-swift draw left them both in a state of complete paralysis. All they could do was stare with a sinking feeling in the pits of their stomachs that told them they had never in all their misspent lives been so close to death. One of them was lean and rawboned. His companion was a burly, unshaven man in a dirty vest.

"Just who do you hombres think I am?" Cassidy demanded.

"It ain't him," the stocky man said swiftly, with brightening face. "Our feller's older and he's got red hair."

"That's right, Bones." The taller of the two men shook his head. "Sorry, mister. When we first saw you we figured you was the hombre we were huntin'. We had our minds dead set on him!"

For an instant Hopalong studied them, then holstered his guns. "Who are you hunting?" he asked curiously.

"Redhead. Hombre's a killer. Shot a cowpoke up north of here. But don't worry, we got him sewed up tighter'n a green hide in the hot sun. Every water hole is blocked, all the trails, and the road to town."

Bones nudged the taller man. "Shut up, Slim! You talk too much!"

Cassidy slung his canteen on the saddle horn, and keeping the horse between himself and the two men, he swung a leg over the saddle. His eyes strayed to the horses the men had been leading. Both of them were marked 8 Boxed H. The 8 preceded the box, the H enclosed. He looked up at the riders and neither of them impressed him favorably. He decided that his sympathies were with the pursued man.

"See you!" he said offhand, then turned the steeldust and rode away. But he sat sideways in the saddle, keeping an eye on the two sullen cowhands.

Slim swallowed and stared at Bones. "You see that hombre throw them guns?" he asked incredulously.

"Stranger around. Wonder if the boss knows him?"

"This hombre looked like Texas to me. Seems maybe I should remember him. . . ."

They walked into the trail, but the unknown gunfighter had already disappeared from view. He was out of their sight, but he had not forgotten them, and right now he was remembering what they had said. . . .

One man alone, water holes guarded, heat, exhaustion, trails blocked, no chance to escape. A man running in smaller and smaller circles until finally trapped. It was not a pleasant thought. He shook his head to clear it of the somber thoughts.

Tascotal should be somewhere ahead, and after that the 3TL. Gibson would be surprised to see him, and as for Connors? He chuckled. Red would have a good laugh when he saw him carrying a repeating Winchester instead of his old single-shot buffalo gun. Red would—

Red?

The man those men had been hunting had been a red-head, older than Hoppy.

Suppose it was Red Connors they were hunting? He pushed on towards town, his eyes and ears alert. He was going to have to hunt up some news.

The lights of Tascotal showed at last; he rode up to the livery stable and swung down. A thin-faced man with sharp eyes came to meet him. He took in Cassidy in one sweeping, comprehensive look, lingering longest on the tied-down guns. "Give him some corn," Hopalong said as the man led the horse towards a stall. "Say, what's going on in this country, anyway? I run into two gents down the road and they sure were hostile."

The stablehand looked at him again, then released the girth on the saddle and slipped it from the horse. "Lucky you didn't get shot, stranger. They are huntin' a mighty salty gent, by all accounts."

"Who is he? What did he do?"

The stablehand spat. "Mister," he said dryly, "you ask a lot of questions and that ain't healthy hereabouts."

"No harm in telling me, is there? I'm interested."

The man hesitated, then shrugged indifferently. "Reckon not. The feller's a stranger who's been out to Gibson's place. Nobody knows what happened, but he run into Ed Springer out on the flatland. There was some shootin', and this hombre downed Ed, then headed back to the 3TL. Some of the Springer outfit took after him, and he cut out for the hills. He's got all the boys scared of his shootin'. He knocked McCale out of the saddle at seven hundred yards with a Winchester. They figure he's out of ammunition now, though, and the boys are closin' in. That's all I know, mister."

Gibson . . . the 3TL . . . a redheaded man who could hit a moving target at just under half a mile! Somewhere out in those black mountains Red Connors was being hunted down like a wild beast.

"Got a fresh horse I could borrow? As good a horse as my gelding?"

The stablehand straightened. "I reckon not. That's a mighty fine horse you got there. Besides," he added, "it's not a good country to be ridin' in now."

"I'll buy a horse. You got one?"

His cold, bright eyes held those of the stablehand for an instant, and then the fellow turned and walked down the line of stalls. In a box stall at the end of the barn was a splendid black horse. As his eyes adjusted to the darkness Hopalong could see a patch of white and gray spots on its flank: an Appaloosa.

"This palouse," the man said, "is the best horse around here. He belongs to an hombre that died mighty sudden here a while back, an' I got a claim against him for the feed bill, so I reckon he's more my horse than anybody's.

"He's a mountain horse and he can outrun, outclimb, outlast any cayuse in this here country. I can't rightly sell him, but I'll mebbe lend him to you on condition you don't tell me where you're goin' or for why. I ain't aimin' to know anythin'."

"Saddle him up!" Hopalong turned to the door. "I'll eat and

pick up some ammunition. You have that horse ready to go, mister."

The stablehand followed Cassidy back and picked up the saddle. As Hopalong started for the door the man's voice stopped him. "Tough country back in there, and those hombres doin' the huntin' know it like the back of their hand, but if I needed a hideout right quick, I reckon I know where I'd go."

Hopalong turned slowly. "Where would that be?"

"There's a cave high up on Copper Mountain, just about timberline. There's water in it, and plenty of wood, and nobody can come close without bein' seen. You hit Lone Pine Pass and turn left up the mountain at the Pine. Keep on the game trail till you get to a blaze-face boulder. Then turn left again and start circlin' the peak. When you cross the rockslide you'll see a clump of trees mebbe five hundred feet higher and what looks like a big ledge. The cave'll be there."

Hopalong's eyes searched the man's face with care. Finally he nodded. "Thanks, friend. I'll remember that."

"Name's Letsinger," the man said. "One time at Doan's Crossin' a feller lookin' somethin' like you sided me in some trouble. Saved my horses for me and kept me and my family from bein' set afoot. I ain't forgettin' that."

"I'm mighty glad I look like that gent you speak of," Hopalong said gravely. "But I sure hope nobody else around here thinks so."

"Reckon nobody would," Letsinger said, "unless it was that man up in the mountains."

CHAPTER 2

Friend in Need

Hopalong Cassidy rode over the top of Coon River Summit. He knew he was striking out blindly and must trust to luck. Yet it was not nearly so much of a guess as it seemed, for he had his knowledge of Red Connors's ways, and his own ability to read sign.

Months ago Hopalong Cassidy had started north to visit his old friend Gibson of the 3TL. Knowing Cassidy was headed that way, Red Connors also had started for the 3TL to meet him, and there their paths were to intersect. They planned, after a short visit, to start on for the Musselshell in Montana.

Now Cassidy had arrived, only to find his friend on the run, perhaps badly wounded, and no word at all of either Gibson, his daughter, or the 3TL. All he knew was that the ranch lay some distance west of these mountains and that there was a possibility that it might also be in trouble. These potentials brought a chill to his heart and a glint of steel to his eyes.

It was nighttime. Until dawn came, neither his knowledge of Red's habits nor his skill at tracking would be of much use in the darkness.

Reaching the summit, he headed downhill and then

turned into the brush and found the trail through the pines that Letsinger, the stablehand, had mentioned.

When he had located Copper Mountain from certain landmarks that Letsinger had mentioned, and had reached the pines fairly well up on the crest, he drew back among some boulders and waited until dawn.

Dawn arrived sooner than he expected, for the night had gone swiftly. He walked out of his hideaway, leading the palouse, and began searching for sign. Almost at once he found the trail of two riders. He backtracked them until suddenly he found the tracks of another horse. He stopped and examined this trail, and after studying it for half a mile he was sure that this was the horse ridden by Red Connors. Obviously the horse was nearly exhausted.

An hour of careful work and Hopalong was coming to the conclusion that Red Connors had not been on the horse at the place where he had first seen its tracks—its path had a random quality that indicated no human intelligence was guiding it. Working back along its trail, searching with greater care, he found the place where the stirrup had dragged when Red carried off the saddle. From there it was but a few minutes until he had found the narrow ledge that led down the brink of the cliff.

Leading the palouse back into the shelter of a grove of aspens, he took his rifle and walked down the path. When he found the place where Red had fainted from loss of blood, he studied the place for a long time. Obviously Red was all in. Hopalong's weather-beaten face became hard and cold. He found the saddle, concealed it, and started on down the path. Soon he found the empty canteen, long dry. Gathering it up, he studied the cliff before him.

Red was trying to get to water, and he would be needing it

badly. Whether he made it or not would be a question, but he was making a try. No matter whether he did or not, he would be closer to the bottom than the top, and it behooved Hopalong to return to the crest, get his horse, and find some way to the base of that cliff.

He had reached the top when he heard footsteps. Stepping back into the shade of a boulder, he saw a man leading his palouse come from the aspens. The man's own horse stood close by. Hopalong drew his gun and waited. The man had a narrow, dark face and looked like a half-breed. The Breed gathered up his own reins and put his foot in the stirrup. In that instant Hopalong stepped from behind the boulder and laid the barrel of his six-shooter behind the Breed's ear. The man crumpled and went down. Hastily, Hopalong gathered him up, stripped him of weapons and ammunition, and then tied him to his horse. Slapping the horse, he started it down the trail, then swung into the saddle himself and turned in the other direction.

It was broad daylight before he finally found a way that showed possibilities of reaching the bottom of the cliff. When he started down he found it was even easier going than he had expected. Off to his right Hoppy could hear a sizable stream running across rocks. Reaching the bottom, he started through the trees, riding slowly.

He passed through a grove of tall pines and then stopped suddenly. Swinging to the ground, he tied his mount and then, rifle in hand, began looking around.

Unless he was much mistaken, this was the place where the trail from above ended, but he found no evidence that Red Connors had ever reached the stream. Climbing a rock for a long view, Hopalong immediately spotted Red and scrambled over the rocks towards him.

He dropped to his knees beside the man, and placed a hand over his heart. Faintly he could feel it beating.

Swiftly he stopped and checked his injured friend for broken limbs. Finding none, he lifted Connors in his arms and made his way to the stream, and then scrambled for his canteen. Carefully he lifted Red's head and touched water to his lips. With his hand he scooped water from the stream and began to bathe Connors's face and head.

The puncher stirred and opened his eyes. He looked up and blinked slowly as he saw Hoppy.

"Reckon," he whispered, "you didn't come none too soon!"

Hopalong made Red as comfortable as possible. Then he uncovered his friend's wounds and examined them. Only one was dangerous. The flesh wound in his side was badly inflamed. Otherwise his trouble had been weakness from thirst and loss of blood. The wound needed attention, and with the few remedies he always carried in his saddlebags Hopalong treated it as well as possible.

Loading Red's rifle and his pistols, he refilled his cartridge belt while keeping a sharp eye on the terrain. This place showed no evidence of visitors, and it was possible that nobody had ever entered the tiny hollow. Where the trail led out to the north he had no idea, and east or west, the walls of the canyon blocked all approach or retreat.

Carefully he scouted the area and returned to find Red fast asleep. Remaining under cover, he scanned the approach to the canyon. There was nothing and no one in sight but the far reaches of the forest, the blue of the distant hills, and no sound but the wind in the trees and the now-distant chuckle of the stream over its rocky bed.

For the time being it appeared they were safe. Unless they stumbled across his trail, nobody would know there was anyone here but Red, and they would probably believe him dead or more badly injured than he had been. Wherever he went, Hopalong found the tracks of a big lion. Evidently it made its den within the area of his search. But there were other tracks. Mule deer were plentiful, and several times he saw sage hens. Seeing a trout leap in the stream, he rigged a line and hooked three in the first thirty minutes. With dry wood gathered from under the pines he built a smokeless fire and began baking the fish. Red was awake when he looked around at him, and Hopalong studied him sourly.

"You sure you're hurt that bad?" he demanded. "Looks to me like you're just taking it easy at my expense. You always were a no-account."

"Me?" Red exploded. "No-account? Why, you lowdown maverickin' coyote! I could work circles around you any day you ever saw, and I've done it many's the time!"

"Yeah?" Hopalong sneered. "When did you ever put in a decent day's work?" Then before Red could make the angry retort that was forming on his lips, Hopalong interrupted, "What's the trouble, anyway? First thing that happens after I get to Tascotal is I hear you're getting yourself shot at. Who's back of this?"

Red grunted, accepting the hot black coffee Hopalong handed him. "Hombre name of Jack Bolt. Has him a brand called the 8 Boxed H."

"That brand don't fool anybody," Hopalong agreed. "Anybody who could handle a running iron could change that over from a 3TL."

"It ain't that simple," Red said. "Nobody has ever killed one of those 8 Boxed H critters to get a look at the inside of the brand, and the job is done so slick I don't see how anybody could burn it with a runnin' iron. I mean, that work is smooth!"

"But they are stealin'?

"Surest thing you know. I spotted a blaze-shouldered steer in their drive and braced 'em about it. They laughed at me and said I was wrong. Then they took me over their range and showed me their tally books, and if they've any extra stock on their range, I sure couldn't find it!"

"So you kept watch?"

"Naturally. I hid out in the hills and watched one big herd. Never saw 'em change a brand or move a head of stock. Then one mornin' as I was about to pull out I saw that herd was a whole durned sight smaller than it had been.

"I hunted around in the hills and couldn't find hide nor hair of 'em, not anywhere. I knowed some of that stock had disappeared, but couldn't see where she'd gone. I hunted around, but all the Bolt hands were on the job.

"Few days later I stumbled on a bunch of tracks 'way back in the hills and started following 'em. Then's when they closed in on me."

"What about Gibson? What's he doing all this time? Sitting on his reservation?"

"Nope. He's laid up with a busted leg. His horse throwed him. Him bein' short-handed like he was, I stayed on and stumbled into this. We'd had a talk, and he told me he was losin' stock, that if it didn't get stopped he'd be cleaned out before he could get back on his feet."

"Where were those cattle headed? You see 'em?"

"Nope. Just the trail. My guess is they are the same cows that slipped out from under my nose while I was watchin' from the hill. But swear to it? I couldn't."

Hopalong nodded thoughtfully. Evidently Red had stumbled upon something hot or there would never have been an attempt to kill him. Did they believe he had trailed them all the way? Was that the reason they were so worried? Or was it because this was the first time anyone was in danger of getting evidence that might lead to conviction?

Hopalong roamed the little valley ceaselessly, worried and restless. Red was in no shape to travel, but they should be moving. If this Jack Bolt had as good a thing here as Red believed, he would not risk the possibility of leaving Red alive. The manhunt would continue until he had been found and killed. In that case, sooner or later they would find this place, and then it would be only a matter of a few hours until they were bottled up tighter than a drum.

He placed several runway snares and within an hour had two rabbits and a sage hen. Returning with these, Hopalong found some silverweed growing along the banks of the stream and gathered some of the roots for roasting. Back at camp, he took time to prepare a good meal from these and some of the supplies he had brought along. When Red awakened again he was hungry. Hopalong looked at him with a sour expression. "I'd sooner buy your clothes than feed you," he said. "You eat like you never expected to again!"

"Mebbe I don't." Red was feeling good and refused battle, even with such a time-honored opponent as Hopalong. "This here Bolt hombre is a tough feller." He looked up suddenly. "You seen Mesquite?"

"Seen him? How could I? He ain't around here, is he?"

"You know wherever you are, he ain't far away. That lad sets a sight o' store by you, Hoppy. Reckon he'll show up?"

Hopalong chuckled and grinned at Red. "Not unless he figures there's trouble over here, but if he gets wind of a scrap, he'll come a-floggin' it. You know him."

As darkness drew nearer, Hopalong became increasingly restless. Red's fever was mounting and there were times when he lapsed into delirium. Hopalong made broth from the sage hen and fed it to the wounded man, then drank some coffee himself.

With Gibson short-handed and laid up with a broken leg, no help was to be expected from that quarter. Moreover, this was far to the east of his holdings, for Red had trailed the stolen cattle for some distance after he found their tracks. Red needed rest and quiet, and before that could be had they must get out of the mountains and down to civilization. Still farther east was the town of Charleston, but from all Hopalong had heard along the trail, that was an outlaw town and a tough one.

A stranger in the vicinity, especially if he wore a badge of any kind or looked like he might represent the law, was sure to draw rifle fire. The inhabitants had long since discovered that one way of keeping their privacy inviolate was scattered shooting at any doubtful-looking stranger. The sheriff who could ride into Charleston and out alive was rare, although there was a rumor that one had done so and lived to brag about it for years. Actually, only a couple of misguided strangers had been found dead. The rest had taken the hint when a few casual rifle shots came too close.

Charleston might be a place to investigate, but that would come later, and it was certainly no place to take Red in his present condition. Other towns were too far away, so that meant a lonely ranch somewhere, or a hideout camp.

CHAPTER 3

A Horse for Red

That night Hopalong bedded down near Red and lay awake, watching and listening. Several times he dipped a cloth in water and placed it across the wounded man's forehead, caring for him as much as he could. Once, when he walked towards the mouth of the canyon, he thought he saw the slinking form of a big cat, and several times an owl hooted. At the canyon mouth all was still. A cricket sounded in the brush, a night bird called, and the wind sounded on the strings of the tall timber.

Red awakened early and stared at Hoppy. "Been awake all night, I bet. You get some sleep. You look like you need it."

Without a word Hopalong rolled up in his blanket and dropped off. Red rolled a smoke and stared at him. Did ever a man have a better friend? All along it had been Hoppy he wanted to see, Hoppy who he knew could pull them out of this, as he had so many times before.

Red's eyes scanned the cliffs. It was unbelievable that he had actually gotten down from there, wounded and only partly conscious, yet he had done it. He had done it and was alive to tell the tale, although had Hopalong not found him he would have been dead for hours now.

Red's mind returned to the trail he had been following when attacked. There had been at least thirty head in that bunch and they had been pushing them fast. None of the riders were known to him and it was a complete mystery where they were headed with the stolen cattle. He suspected all were recently rebranded 3TL steers—ample evidence to stretch a few necks if delivered to the right sources.

They would never rest now until they had him. A cowboy named Grat had been in that crowd before the cattle were delivered to the strange riders. He knew the horse he rode and had followed its tracks more than once, often on Jack Bolt's range.

He checked his rifle and grinned when he saw it was loaded. He threw sticks on the fire and, without moving from his propped-up position, succeeded in getting the fire going and the coffee on. It was boiling when Hopalong opened his eyes and came awake.

Hopalong Cassidy checked his guns and belted them on, then accepted the cup Red offered him. "You look better," he said at last. "I'm going to leave you in this hideaway. Nobody seems to have come here for years, and if they do, you're well hid. The trees and rocks give you cover, and you're sure not going to let many of 'em get close with that rifle."

"Where you goin'?" Red demanded.

"To get you a cayuse. You can't walk out of here, and I'm not going to load my horse down with your carcass."

Red snorted and Hopalong swung into the saddle of the palouse and started off. Leaving the canyon, he took to the rocks, careful to leave no trail. In so doing he looked for his incoming tracks but found none.

It was an hour later when he found fresh tracks of the

cordon of riders that had been beating the canyons and valleys for Red Connors. The tracks looked less than an hour old, as nearly as he could judge, and they led down along the mountainside through the trees.

Four riders were gathered over the ashes of a fire under the shade of a huge slab of granite. One of them he recognized at once, from the description Red had given, as Grat. Big, rough-looking, Grat was leaning against a rock, smoking a cigarette.

"The devil with it!" Grat was saying. "He's dead or gone out of the country!"

"Well, someone slugged the Breed here," Bones explained. "But I don't think it was our fella. Anyway, what difference does it make? If we go back, we'll be ridin' fence and brandin' cows. This here ain't a bad life."

The others were a dark-faced man who wore his hat high over a makeshift bandage on the back of his head—Hoppy recognized him as the man he had hit with his pistol—and Hoyt, who had been one of the watchers left on the crest after Red had disappeared.

Hopalong circled warily up the hillside behind them, then left his horse and worked his way down through the trees towards the rustlers' camp. He had heard a few words and wanted to hear more, but he also wanted a bay that he could see picketed about twenty-five yards downhill from where the men were relaxing. On second thought he picked a gray. At a distance that bay might look enough like a sorrel to warrant investigation, and he wanted no trouble while Red was wounded.

He studied the four men individually and found them true to type. All were tough-looking, all packed guns low, and all looked like men accustomed to using them. If this was the brand of men Jack Bolt had doing his rustling, they were no pushovers in any kind of a scrap.

Nobody spoke for a few minutes. Hoyt was lying on the ground now, his head pillowed on his sombrero. He drew deep on his cigarette and looked up at the blue sky and idly drifting clouds.

"The boss said he was takin' a couple of us into Tascotal tonight," he said. "I hope it ain't me. This is the first rest I've had in months."

"I could go for some of that panther sweat they sell in there," Bones said thoughtfully. "This ridin' is mighty dry work."

Hopalong had moved down now within pistol shot of the horses, who were beyond the riders in a grove of trees. With infinite care, and taking all the time in the world, he eased himself through the trees and reached the picket rope of the grey. The horse jerked his head up, and Hopalong spoke gently to him. Curiously, the horse came nearer, and Hopalong murmured to him and scratched his shoulder, then his chest near the foreleg. The grey liked it, and after a minute or so Hopalong turned and led the grey back into the trees and tied him. Returning, he released the other horses. They seemed ready to go, and began drifting off.

Mounting his own horse and leading the grey, Hopalong allowed his tracks to merge with the others in the trail, then cut off the traveled way, keeping to the flat rock of the country alongside the road and moving from one wide, wind-swept rock shelf to another until he had put a half mile between himself and the camp.

After a couple of miles he cut off through the timber towards the canyon. Several times he made abrupt turns; once he made almost a complete circle, working his way farther back into the hills. It was almost sundown when he reached the canyon.

Red looked at him and grinned as he came up. "Saw you comin'," he said. "You got a horse."

"What did you want—a cow? Although," he added dryly, "she might be easier for you to ride."

"Huh! I can ride anythin' you can put a saddle on!" Red bristled. "I've seen you get piled a few times!"

"You dream a lot!" Hopalong looked at him critically. "You figure you can stay in that saddle if I put you there?"

"Try me!" Red hitched his way along the ground. "Let me get a hand on that stirrup and I'll get in the saddle by myself."

"And get your head kicked off!" Hopalong replied.

When Red Connors was in the saddle he grinned at Hoppy. "There was a time back there when I didn't know whether I'd ever get up here again," he said. "I figured maybe they had my number up at last."

"Let's go!" Leading the way, Hopalong started down the canyon. They were careful to leave no tracks and once out of the woods near the canyon, Hopalong turned back into the higher mountains towards the north. At all costs, even at the risk of a longer ride, they must avoid trouble. Red was in no shape for a fight right now.

"What about this Jack Bolt, Red? Know anything about him?"

"Only what Gibson told me. He came in here about four years ago with two riders and bought a small spread. He paid cash for it, I hear, and the owner who sold to him left town right after. Seems somethin' happened to him, because a year later they found what was left of him over near the Bruneau. He was long dead, just his skeleton and a few rags of clothes.

They identified him by his boots and some letters in his leather jacket.

"Nobody seems to have thought anything about that, including Gibson. Lately, however, he's been wonderin' if that feller Newcombe wasn't followed away and killed.

"Bolt went to ranchin' an' stayed away from town most of the first year. When he started comin' around, it was just to buy supplies, and he acted like a quiet, peaceful rancher. Then two rough-looking hombres hit town askin' for him, and they went to work as hands. One of them was this Grat, who's with him now. The other was Bones. Bolt, he got mighty friendly with that tough Springer outfit, but trouble didn't start until Grat pulled in.

"It was about that time folks began to miss a few cows. Bolt complained, too, but not until there had been some talk by others. Then Bolt went to the sheriff an' told him he was missin' stock. For a while the sheriff investigated, but nobody lost any stuff for several weeks, and then Fielding of the 3F came up with a lot of stock missin'."

"That 3F would make an 8 Boxed H, too," Hopalong commented. "How about the other brands?"

"It will cover more than half the brands in this neck of the woods," Red said emphatically. "And you wonder why somebody ain't pointed it out? A feller named Brown sure tried it. He said it right out in meeting before Grat, and Grat told him if he said the Bolt outfit were thieves, he was a liar!"

"And Brown grabbed iron?"

"Don't reckon he meant to. I just heard about it. He said somethin', and I figure he aimed to claim he was just mentionin' the fact, but Grat called him a liar again, and that time he reached. He never got his gun clear. Grat downed him."

"And since then no comment, huh?"

"That's right, Hoppy. Bolt's kept a good reputation some-how, and there's only a few who think he's anythin' but honest. None of them cotton to his outfit too much, but nobody will come out and call 'em thieves."

CHAPTER 4

Rustler Plans

$\mathbf{J}$ack Bolt had every reason to feel satisfied. In the seven months of rustling, his hands had stolen over a thousand head of cattle from ranches within a day's ride of his 8 Boxed H. All but fifty head of those cattle were safely out of the country, transferred to another ranch he now owned in northern California.

With only six hands doing the rustling, the split was small, and not one of the six had any idea how he disposed of the cattle. At a certain point on the trail the herds were turned over to other men, who drove them north, then west. Only one herd had followed the trail discovered by Red Connors and that had gone to the mining camps of Western Montana for the purpose of immediate cash. Most of the returns had gone to the six cowhands.

Bolt sat in a hide-bound armchair on his veranda and contemplated the situation. Gibson was down with a broken leg but would be out and around soon. If a big strike was to be made, it should be now. With Red Connors out of the way, the one man who knew anything definite had been eliminated, and the chances were, people would believe he had drifted out of the country as he had come in.

Bolt was very well pleased. The whole job had been handled simply but effectively and without any suspicion being directed towards him. There had been a little talk when Grat killed Brown, but Grat was only considered overhasty and was not otherwise under suspicion. Bolt had been careful to report small losses of cattle from time to time and, while making the usual complaints, had suggested the losses could also have been from straying, varmints, or lack of water.

Jack Bolt was a tall man, well over six feet, and slightly stooped. His shoulders were narrow and rounded, his face long and saturnine, narrow through the cheekbones but wide at the jaw. His hide was browned like saddle leather, and his large nose jutted from between close-set black eyes. The hand that held his pipe was large, with prominent knuckles.

Although he gave little evidence of it, he was a man of some education and he had begun life with large ideas, which expanded into grandiose plans, but plans that always waited for the lucky strike he expected to make, the big killing. At forty he was an embittered man who blamed the world for the success that had never come to him, failing to understand that the fault was his own. He was one of those who had always wanted to start at the top, and the idea of consistent effort to get there had seemed futile to him.

His first break with the law had come when he was twenty-six and traveling with two hard-case hands. They convinced him that a stage holdup would net them all a stake, and he had fallen in with the plan. He had been badly frightened, nervous, and jumpy. He had fired the shot that killed a passenger with his hands in the air.

The dispute with his partners that followed angered him

because of their contempt, and while one of them was away from camp he had murdered the other and fled with the money. Attempting to build the six hundred dollars taken from the stage into a big stake, he had lost it all.

In the following years he had been a stage driver, buffalo hunter, and livestock buyer, occasionally rustling small bunches of cattle and still hoping for the big break when somebody would recognize his sterling qualities and present him with a top job and much money, or someone would fall dead after making him the heir to millions. None of it ever happened, as it never does to those who expect and hope for it, and at last he had settled down to real effort.

By that time he had the reputation of a hard man to handle. The killings that began his criminal career had been only two of many. There had been a man he killed in Caldwell, and another in Denver. In a poker game he won a few thousand dollars and had moved into the country where he now was and bought a small ranch and some cattle. With extreme care, for he now had his big plan started, he rustled a few cows, never letting his herd grow large, keeping his sale herds small but fat. By the same methods he was using, even without the rustling, he could in a few years have become honestly prosperous. But he had no such intention.

On a trip north he had swung off the main trail and, in the mountains of California, had found a valley, built a cabin, and hired a couple of cowhands who wanted nothing so much as plenty to eat and a place to sleep. In the neighborhood he purchased a few cattle and a half-dozen horses.

By the time he was ready to branch out he was well known around Tascotal, but nobody knew of the California ranch. He had picked up six cowhands whom he had carefully watched and tested, and then he began operations. At the end of seven months his own ranch showed only the natural increase, but the ranch in California was running a thousand head and he had acquired four more hands on that end.

It was his nature to grow impatient. Thus far he had been slow, painstaking, and careful in the extreme. The plan had worked without a flaw. Until the coming of Red Connors, a cattle- and trail-wise veteran of many rustler campaigns, there had been no suspicion, and the losses had been so carefully scattered that many were still not convinced any rustling was taking place. Now he wanted to clean up fast. He wanted San Francisco, the bright lights and an easier life. And the quickest way was a sudden wholesale steal of cattle from the 3TL.

Grat drifted into the yard and swung down from a weary horse. Stripping the saddle from the animal, he turned it into the corral and then stamped up to the porch, beating the dust from his hat against one leg of his chaps.

"Ain't found him," Grat said. "Durned fool dropped plumb out of sight."

"That country closed up yet?" Bolt demanded sharply.

"Sure is! We used them Aragon boys, like you said, and bottled up every trail, watched every water hole." Grat had decided not to mention that he and the others had spent most of the afternoon chasing down horses that had mysteriously wandered off or the fact that some unknown person had hung a knot on the back of the Breed's head. The men were still out looking and he hoped they'd have Connors pinned down or dead by tomorrow at the latest.

"We found that sorrel he was ridin', and there was blood on the horse's withers. He's bad hurt and the boys are closing in on him. Only thing that worries me: a man could lose himself back in there and die and might never be found."

Jack Bolt scowled. "You make sure you find him, or his

body. He was from that old Bar 20 outfit, and they were plumb salty. I want to know he's dead, no maybes!"

Grat nodded. He was in complete agreement with that idea. So far this whole affair had gone off smoothly, increasing his respect for Bolt. His own inclinations had been to start rustling big, but now he realized that the other man's idea had been much the best.

"See anybody out on the trail?" Bolt asked. "Anybody from Tascotal?"

"Nary a soul." Grat leaned back and rolled a smoke, staring out over the dancing heat-waves in the valley. "You figurin' on a drive?"

"Uh-huh. Gibson's still got that fat stock back in the canyon. There must be three hundred head there."

Grat grinned. "Now you're talkin'! Let's get after some big herds! We could have a thousand head of cattle out of here in three weeks with the right kind of breaks, and another thousand before they could get organized to try stoppin' us."

"All right. Figure on it for night after tomorrow. Call a couple of men in and get them rested up. We'll head right north and make a straight drive of thirty miles before we stop. A few hours' rest, then twenty more. If they are tired they'll be easier to handle."

Grat got to his feet. "All right." He hesitated. "Say, Bones wanted me to ask if it would be all right for him to ride into town. Him and Sim Aragon—"

"No!" Jack Bolt's face hardened with irritation. "You know better than that! I don't want any of you seen with those Aragon boys, do you hear? They got a bad rep around here. I want to keep you boys clean in this country. If he wants to go to town, he can go alone, but not with Sim. And if he does go, he's to hobble his lip. He talks too much when he's drinkin'."

Grat shrugged. "Don't blame me! He said to ask."

"You've asked. If we start perambulatin' around town with that no-account Aragon outfit, the first thing people will be findin' us about as welcome as a polecat at a picnic! The Aragons are plumb mean. Sim killed a man in Tascotal only about a month ago, and for durned little reason, from all I hear."

Grat walked out and roped and saddled a horse. Bones would not like it, but the boss was right, nevertheless. This had been the most peaceful rustling he had ever done; not a shot fired, not a doubt raised. Why, it could go on for years, maybe!

For years? He suddenly realized he was already tired of it. Too much like regular work. It was time to make a big clean-up and get out, and apparently that was what the boss thought, too.

Tascotal drowsed in the warmth of a noonday sun. Flies buzzed lazily and the horses stamped in the dust. The sound of boots on the boardwalk was pleasant to hear, and the lazy voices of men making cow-town conversation, casual shoptalk, and easy jokes that drew smiles rather than laughter.

A buckboard's wheels creaked as it slowed before the hitch rail in Higgins' Emporium. Sue Gibson got down, and the men looked up with the interest always drawn by a pretty girl stepping out of a vehicle.

"Howdy, ma'am! How's your pa?" One of the men drawled a polite, lazy question.

She looked around with a quick smile. Her red-gold hair accompanied a ready, friendly expression and there were a few freckles over her nose.

"He's better," she replied, "but more trouble to me! He thinks he should be out looking after his cattle. He's worried about rustlers."

"Aw! That's all talk, Miss Sue! Come late spring they always start to head back in the hills like this! Tell him not to worry none."

"Is Red Connors around town?" she asked. "He left suddenly and we haven't seen him."

"We ain't seen him neither," another man spoke up, his eyes alert with interest. "We figured he'd be around awhile, the way he talked."

Sue hesitated. "If you see him, let us know. He left his horse at the ranch and took off riding a sorrel of Dad's. Most of his outfit is there, too."

Grat was lounging in front of the saloon, a big, hard-faced man, waiting for Bones to get into town with Sim so he could warn him of what the boss had said. He had given Bones his permission to come on in, thinking it would be all right with Bolt. Now he was worried, for Jack Bolt meant what he said, and Grat could see the sense in the order.

He walked down the boardwalk towards Sue Gibson. "Howdy, ma'am! Heard you speakin' about that Connors feller. I reckon he sloped it. One of the boys met him 'way east of here, and he said he was headin' for Montany."

"Montana?" Sue frowned. "But he wouldn't do that! I know one of his old outfit has a ranch up there, but he'd not leave when he knew Hopalong was coming!"

Grat stiffened. It took him a minute to get his voice calm so he could speak. "Did you say Hopalong? You mean Hopalong Cassidy?"

"Why, yes! I suppose you've heard of him." Sue looked at Grat, somewhat surprised at the reaction to her statement. "He and Red rode together for a long time. They were to meet here."

At once Grat knew panic. If Hopalong was coming this way, Bolt should know it at once. Notorious for his willingness to do battle on any and all occasions, Cassidy had a wide reputation for disliking rustlers. It was no time to rustle that herd of Gibson's.

"When was he supposed to arrive?" he asked casually.

"Why, he's overdue, and Dad wanted to see him very much. I thought maybe he and Red had gotten together here in town and were having a good time before they came to the ranch."

Grat shoved his hat on the back of his head and rubbed his unshaven jaw as he stared down the street. For once he did not turn to watch Sue walk into the store. He was worried and angry. This would have to happen just when they were about to make a clean-up so he could get out of the country! Now everything would be delayed!

But would it? Suppose Hopalong never got here? Suppose he was dry-gulched on the way? If Aragon heard about it, then it would not be his fault if Sim took it on himself to kill Hopalong, and there was nothing that he would like better, Grat knew. That was it—he would tell Sim. And Aragon was due in town at any minute.

Somewhat relieved by the decision, Grat leaned against the awning pole and waited, smoking two cigarettes before he saw them ride into town: the rotund Bones and the lean-featured, tigerlike Aragon.

Both men swung down in front of the saloon, and Grat stepped between the horses and passed on his information. Sim Aragon's eyes lighted with excitement. A vicious killer he might be, but he was not a coward. A vain man, he could see how people would fear him if he killed the famous gunslinger of the Bar 20. Bones's face had gone blank with shock, and Grat was struck by something in his expression.

"What's the matter?" he demanded sharply.

"Grat"—Bones's lips fumbled with the words—"that hombre Hopalong Cassidy was a friend of Red Connors. Cassidy will be plenty sore if Connors is dead."

Sim Aragon laughed. "Why be worried? He's only one man! I'll take care of him!"

"You can have him!" Bones whispered fervently. "I want nothin' to do with that hombre!"

Grat had forgotten what Bolt had advised, and the three trooped into the saloon together. One of the men who had spoken to Sue Gibson looked after them, his brow furrowed. "Now, that's funny!" he said to the man beside him. "I'd never figure any of Bolt's boys to be hangin' out with a thief like Aragon!"

"Aw, just rode in with him, maybe. I did it myself, few days back." He spat. "Can't say I liked it, neither."

"Yeah, that could be it." The tall puncher got to his feet. "Think I'll have a drink." He scowled. There had been something furtive about them as they talked, and he had heard Grat swearing. Now what was that about? Stopping short, he went into the Emporium.

"Miss Sue," he said apologetically, "could I ask you somethin'?"

She turned quickly, a surprised smile on her face. These men were always most polite, but few of them had ever gone out of their way to address her. "Why, certainly, Joe. What is it?"

"Seems sort of strange to me, and it sure ain't none of my business, but what did you tell Grat just now?"

"Grat? Oh! Why, not much of anything! He just said he thought Red had gone on out of the country, and I told him that wouldn't be true because Red knew Hopalong Cassidy was coming up to meet him."

"Cassidy?" Joe stared at her, an idea slowly forming in his brain. "Now what do you know about that?"

"Why do you ask, Joe? What happened?"

"Why, Grat seemed plumb upset about something, and then that Bones feller come in ridin' with Sim Aragon, and he couldn't get to them fast enough to tell 'em. Then Bones told Grat somethin' and he fell to cussin' somethin' awful. I reckon," he added, "I'm makin' a lot out of nothin', but it doesn't look right, and them with Aragon, too."

"No," Sue replied slowly, "it doesn't."

Sue looked at Joe. She knew the man by sight and had even danced with him once at a social. Joe Gamble rode for the 3F outfit. He was an honest, hard-working man and a top hand. "Joe," she asked suddenly, "have you lost any cattle lately?"

It was his turn to look sharply at her, his eyes suddenly alert. "We sure have, ma'am. Hard to say how many, but some."

"So have we. Red thought he had found a trail that morning he rode off. He said nothing to anyone else and told me not to tell Dad—it might worry him. He said he would follow it up, then come back. That was days ago, and there has been no sign of him since."

Joe Gamble absorbed that slowly. He frowned at his boot toes. It was all vague and made no sense. None of them really knew they had lost cattle, and it might be they were heading into higher country where there was more water and the grass was greener. It could be. Still, when a man has been on the range for years he comes to the point where he can judge the number of cattle very well, and he was positive they were losing stock. Now Sue Gibson said Red had had the same suspicion. How about the others? It would do no harm to ask around.

"May be nothin' to it," he commented then, "but if this here Hopalong shows up, let me know, will you? I may," he added, "scout around and try to pick up Red's trail. He seemed like a right nice feller."

"We—Dad, I mean—have known Red Connors for a long time, and Hopalong, too. They drove herds over the trail together. They were together when my husband was killed."

"Your husband?" Joe Gamble was startled. None of them had any idea Sue Gibson had been married, let alone that she was a widow.

"Yes, I was married to Luke Potter. After he died I started using my own name again, as Dad wanted me to. Luke was a fine man."

Back out on the store porch Gamble shook his head and smiled to himself. Women were always a surprise, he thought. It was best, he realized, never to think you had a handle on one of them, because you were always sure to be wrong.

At the bar, over whiskey, the three owlhoots had reached some conclusions. "He smelled somethin', that's what. He's up in those hills somewheres now, scoutin' for Connors."

"Maybe he's found him already." Grat was thinking of the gray horse that Hoyt had been riding . . . the one that was still missing.

Sim Aragon downed his whiskey and shoved back in his chair. "You tell Jack he needn't worry about Cassidy. I'll pick up my outfit and we'll go through them hills so careful we could find any rabbit and squirrel in the place. We'll find those two, and when we do, Jack's trouble regardin' them'll be over."

After Sim was gone, Grat looked across the table at Bones. He shook his head. "Too good to last! I knowed it. I hate to tell Jack. He'll raise the roof."

Bones looked like a soiled cupid, his round face heavy with knowledge of a chance lost. "That musta been Cassidy we seen at White Rock. We could've bushed him," he said, "if we knowed."

CHAPTER 5

Ranch Spy

Copper Mountain's Cave was exactly where Letsinger had advised Hoppy. It was after dark when Red Connors and he made it, but once at the mouth, Hopalong took time to investigate the terrain as thoroughly as possible. The cave was big, and pack rats had dragged in huge piles of dead brush to make nests. They offered a good supply of kindling.

When he had a fire going and Red was bedded down, Hopalong examined his friend's wound. It looked bad, and obviously the long day's ride had done it no good at all. After bathing the wound and dressing it once more, Hopalong returned to the fire and got busy with supper. The horses had been unsaddled and picketed on grass in the nearby woods. The grass was thick, and as little game and no stock came up this high, it was undisturbed. The fire was well back into the cave, and the mouth was concealed anyway by the wall formed by the stand of trees.

"Gibson's the only one who's been very suspicious of Bolt, and he may be wrong," Red offered suddenly. "Until I followed this trail, there was no evidence of any kind against him. It might be just that Aragon outfit."

"Heard of them. Three of 'em, aren't there?"

"Uh-huh. And they got three or four gents ridin' with 'em. Rough crowd. Reminds me of that bunch Nevady had down south, that time. Sim's the boss. He's a long, thin galoot who fancies himself with a gun. He's purty good, too. Pete and Manuel are the other two. Both of 'em plumb salty."

"They run with the Bolt outfit?"

"Not so's you'd notice. Nobody likes the Aragons. Poison mean. They'd as soon shoot you as look at you."

"Red," Hopalong said as they were eating, "there's grub enough here for several days. You've got plenty of firewood without moving to get it, and your horse will do all right on that grass. There's water back in the cave, and I notice that there's some rain in a pool outside that'll do your cayuse."

"All of which means you're pullin' your freight?" Red grinned at him. "Shucks, Hoppy, hit the trail! I can get along, and Gibson will be needin' help."

"Well, I think you'll be all right," Hopalong said. "At least until I can get back or send someone for you."

Rolling up in his blankets, Hopalong tried to get to sleep. Red Connors stared at him and grinned. Not for the world would he have hinted to his old friend how good it was to have him back, but now there would be little to worry about, for the famous gunman could always, in his experience, outfigure and outshoot anybody who came along the pike. With the first sense of comfort he had felt in days, Red Connors stretched out and was soon asleep. When he awakened, the first gray of day was appearing far off over the mountains. Hopalong Cassidy was already gone.

.　.　.

Before Hopalong lay a vast sweep of sunken gorges and towering peaks, most of them timber-clad, but gradually growing less so towards the west until, near the area where the 3TL lay, the hills were almost without a tree. That country to the west was barren and showed no sign of water, yet Hopalong knew it was there—if a man knew how to find it.

Below him all was dark and still. The stars were bright overhead, and the hint of dawn lay along the sky far away, a thin spreading gray in the east. The palouse took to the trail with ears pricked up, eager to be going. Angling across the mountain, Hopalong found a way into the forest and slowly worked his way farther and farther down the slope. Tascotal lay off to the south and west, but he intended to hold to the wilder country as long as he could before breaking into the open where he might be seen.

The 3TL lay in a corner of the hills and among a pleasant grove of cottonwood. There were the usual scattered outbuildings, in better shape than most, several corrals, and a green patch that might be a lawn. Nearer, Hopalong saw that it was not only a lawn but there were flowers. He dismounted, wanting to look around before he went inside, but there was no chance of that. There was a call from the door, and he turned to see a girl waving from the steps. Her hair caught the morning sun and gleamed red and gold. For an instant Hopalong's cold blue eyes lit, and then he dropped the reins of his palouse, who promptly walked off towards the watering trough, and strode towards the girl.

Her eyes bright with curiosity, she looked up at this man of whom she had heard so much. In Texas, as a little girl, she had heard of him and of the fabled Bar 20 and the Double Y, which succeeded it as the hangout of the old Bar 20 outfit. She saw the weather-beaten face, the sloping shoulders, his friendly smile, and then her eyes fell to the two bone-handled Colts tied down to his legs. These guns had killed more than one man.

"Hoppy?" she asked expectantly. "You are Hopalong, aren't you?"

"Sure am! And you're Sue Gibson—or is it Potter?"

"Gibson. Did you know Luke?"

"Never did." He did not say that he had seen him once; Luke Potter had been lying trampled in the mud beside his saddle. The girth had broken when he was trying to head off a stampede. "Your dad getting along all right?"

"Yes, he's dying to see you, Hoppy! He's done nothing but talk about you since he first heard you were coming." She looked up quickly. "Red's not here. He rode off and hasn't come back."

"I know. I've seen him."

A stumpy rider with a deep chest who lounged in the shade of the blacksmith shop got up quickly and walked towards his horse. He swung into the saddle and started off. After a moment Hopalong heard the sound of the horse beginning to run. He stopped in the doorway, his eyes straying towards the sound. "How many of your boys here now?" he asked.

"Why, only two!" Sue was surprised. "Frank Gillespie and Pod Griffin. Why do you ask?"

"Been with you long?"

"Frank has. He rode in here with Dad. He was with him on that same drive where you met Father. Pod? Well, he's been with us three or four months, maybe a little more."

"Go find out if they are still there, will you, ma'am? As a favor to me?" He smiled. "I think Pod will be gone off somewheres."

She started away from him, and removing his hat, Hopalong shoved his damp white hair back from his brow and started into the house, where Gibson was calling him.

The older man was propped up in bed, a big man with a kindly face topped off with bristly gray hair. His smile was wide. "Hoppy! You old son of a gun! Sure is good to see yuh!"

"Better than last time?" Hopalong chuckled. "Last time I remember you figured maybe I was lyin' to you about having my herd sold."

Gibson chuckled. "Well, wouldn't you have been suspicious? That story sounded mighty old. Just the same, tough as they was, I'd like to take a herd over that trail again!"

"You wouldn't like it now." Hopalong dropped into a chair. "Fact is, she's almost gone. Too many fences. An hombre was plowing up a field sixty miles north of Doan's Crossin' last time I come through. First time I ever saw that country was over the sights of a Sharps with Injuns coming a-whooping. She sure has changed."

Sue came in and paused in the door. "Pod's rode off somewhere," she said, looking curiously at Hopalong. "How did you know?"

"Read it in my crystal ball." He smiled. "I reckon he's gone off to tell somebody I'm here. Somebody who's rustling cows."

"Oh, no!" Sue objected. "Not Pod!"

Hopalong shrugged. "Perhaps not, but I'd be mighty curious why else a man races out of here this time of day running his horse, and just after I arrived. Looks strange to me."

"He's sort of peculiar, that one," Gibson admitted. "Acts like he was raised on sour milk."

Briefly, then, Hopalong covered the events of his arrival at Tascotal, and his earlier meeting with Slim and Bones at White Rock Wells, and how they had mistaken him for a man they were hunting. Their further comments had led him to believe that that man was Red Connors.

"You eat yet?" Gibson asked. "Fix him somethin', Sue. Cook's gone to town," he added, "buyin' supplies."

Sue led the way to the kitchen and got down some cold beef, beans, and some biscuits. "They are huckydummy," she said. "But if I catch you picking the raisins out and eating them without bread, I'll scorch you!"

Hopalong grinned. "Easy to tell you were raised on a cow ranch," he said. "That's an old trick."

"Not on this ranch it isn't!" Sue was positive. Then she turned to the cupboard and took out a large apple pie cut in four pieces. "I don't suppose you could eat more than two pieces of this pie?"

"Well"—he studied the pie seriously—"I don't know, but I doubt if I could eat less."

"If you want more than that you'll fight Dad for his share." She winked at Hoppy.

"I'll just have to make do." Hopalong grinned. "Although, since we've got a sick man here, I don't know that he'll have enough appetite for that other half."

"You just watch me, Cassidy! You just watch!"

They all laughed, but then Hopalong became serious. "Is there someone you could send up to Copper Mountain to check on Red? He's a tough old bird but I'm worried about him." Gibson appeared to think for a moment and Hopalong went on: "I think whoever it is should be from town or one of your neighbor's ranches. I don't trust this man Pod, an' you're going to need your other hand right here."

"Joe Gamble." Sue said immediately. "He rides for the 3F and he's worried about rustling just like we are."

"She's right. Joe's a good boy," Gibson agreed.

"All right, can you get word to him?"

"First thing in the morning," Sue said as she put a pot on the stove.

While the coffee was heating, Hopalong got busy on the beef and beans. While he was eating, a horse came into the yard, and Sue's eyes grew darker. "That's probably Pod come back."

"How far could he ride in that time?" Hoppy asked. "As far as the 8 Boxed H?"

Sue nodded, her eyes flashing. "That's about the only place he could ride, unless he met somebody in the hills."

"Possibly," Hopalong suggested, "I should have a talk with him."

Yet he remained, talking to Sue and then to her father about the country, listening to their descriptions of places and people, knowing that every comment might someday be vital, for they knew this country as he did not. It was after ten when he finally got to his feet. There was still a light in the bunkhouse. Saying good night, he walked outside.

Carelessly, without a glance towards the bunkhouse, he strolled down to the corrals, but had hardly rounded the corner of the corral before a boot grated on gravel behind him. Wheeling, Hopalong was just in time to catch Pod grabbing for his gun.

Cassidy sidestepped quickly and flashed his Colt. It spat flame, and Pod sprang back, gripping his bloody wrist and swearing.

Hopalong closed in instantly, hearing a door slam at the house and then from the bunkhouse. Pod stared at him, his eyes ugly in the dim light from the window.

"You durned near shot my hand off!" he exclaimed.

Cassidy picked up the fallen pistol, then spun the man

around and started him towards the house. Sue stood in the doorway, a shotgun in her hands. Frank Gillespie had come from the bunkhouse with a Winchester.

"Got him, huh?" Gillespie stared from Cassidy to Pod. "I figured he was up to somethin'. Usually he can't get to sleep too soon, but tonight he sat up and kept sittin' up. I was keepin' an eye on him, but sort of dozed off."

"Better go back in the house, Sue," Hopalong said quietly. "We got us a job to do."

She was close to him now, but evidently what she saw in his eyes reassured her, for she turned and walked back to the house. When the door slammed, Hoppy motioned to Frank.

"Get a rope," he said. "This hombre's horse'll be saddled, so we'll use it. That cottonwood over there ought to do the job."

Pod's face went white as death. "Hey! You ain't goin' to hang me? You can't do that!"

"No?" Hopalong's voice was icy. "Why not? You're workin' with rustlers, aren't you? You sold out your boss, didn't you? You tried to shoot me in the back, didn't you? What do you expect?"

Terror flooded the man's features. "No!" He almost screamed the word. "Don't hang me—don't! I didn't mean it!"

"All right, then," Hopalong replied reasonably. "Tell us who you are working for and what the setup is."

"They'd kill me!" Pod protested.

Hopalong's chuckle was unpleasant. "Rather get it from them or us? Perhaps they'll shoot you, but I promise, if you don't talk, I'll hang you!"

Pod hesitated, desperately searching for some way out, but the faces of the two men convinced him. Frank Gillespie had neither liked nor trusted him, and as for Cassidy—

"All right," Pod said hoarsely. "It was"—he hesitated, and

a crafty light came into his eyes—"it was the Aragons. They are
the rustlers. They tried to kill your friend Red Connors, and
wanted to get you. They didn't set me on to it, though," he
added honestly enough. "I figured I'd do it on my own."

"Aragon?" Hopalong stared at the man, trying to see his
eyes better. It was difficult to tell whether the man was telling
the truth or not, but it sounded like he was lying. "You sure?"

"Who else could it be?" Pod demanded. "I should know,
shouldn't I?"

"It might be Jack Bolt," Hopalong said calmly. "It might be
those hands of his—Grat, Bones, and the rest."

"Don't know how you'd figure it was them," Pod said. "I
don't know 'em at all."

"You lie!" Gillespie said harshly. "I saw you with 'em more
than once! You and that Grat are thicker than thieves! Haul on
that rope, Hoppy. Let's hang this hombre!"

"No!" Pod gasped hoarsely. "Don't hang me! It was Bolt!
He's in with Aragon! They are hittin' your north herd tonight!"

"What?" Gillespie roared. "Tonight?"

"Take the rope off him," Hopalong said quietly. "Then go
saddle up."

"You lettin' him go?" Gillespie was incredulous.

"He talked, and I'm lettin' him go. If I ever see him again
I'll start shooting on sight. Hear that, you coyote?"

"I hear it." Pod was sullen, still unbelieving of his luck.

"All right, get goin'!"

Pod sprang into the saddle and raced for the trail; then his
hand dropped to the rifle scabbard, viciousness mounting
within him. "I'll kill that sidewinder!" he growled. His hand
struck emptiness. He grabbed again, but his Winchester was
gone. Hopalong had quietly slipped it from the scabbard.

Swinging from the trail, Pod slapped the spurs into his

mount. There was still time. He might beat them to the herd and warn Jack Bolt. And when he did he would get a rifle and take care of that Cassidy. Make him talk, would they? All the innate viciousness within him surged to the fore. He had been forced to crawl, made to show that deep streak of yellow that lay within him, and the knowledge of his action brought out all the evil in his nature.

They would see. He was not through. Just wait until he got a gun!

CHAPTER 6

Agate

As the two riders raced for the holding ground Hopalong's thoughts were busy. Actually there was no substantial evidence against Jack Bolt—or the Aragons, for that matter. They were suspected, and Red Connors had found a trail that might have led to something definite, but he had been wounded and the trail lost. Pod had talked, but he was not a man who could be relied upon in any case. What was needed now was to catch them in the act or find some convincing evidence of their crookedness.

Even the trail Red had found did not begin at the 8 Boxed H, but back in the hills, and would not be accepted in any court. It was one thing to know an outfit was rustling, but quite another thing to prove it, and proof would be needed, for Jack Bolt was unsuspected by most of the cattlemen in the area. According to Red and what others he had found time to talk to, Bolt's herds had not been increasing at an unusual rate. Obviously the cattle were being speedily taken out of the country or held somewhere out of sight.

The moon was rising when they crossed the saddle at breakneck speed and drew up in the valley below. The air was heavy with the smell of dust and of cattle, but there was not an animal in sight. Faintly, Hopalong could see the tracks of the herd moving off to the north. Walking his horse and leaning far over in the saddle to watch the trail, he led off.

After a few minutes he could see that the cattle were headed towards a break in the hills before them, and he slipped his rifle from the scabbard and drew up. "Frank," he asked quietly, "you know this country?"

"Most of it. That country north and west is bone-dry as far's I know. It sure ain't good cow country."

Hoppy nodded. "Bone-dry? Ever hear of High Rock Canyon?"

"Uh-huh, but never been there. That's a long way over west. This outfit's headed north. There's no water either way so far as I know."

"There's water in High Rock," Hopalong said. "Feller told me so some years back. The wagon outfits used to go through that way to Oregon and northern California. There's a few scattered streams over that way, too."

Gillespie agreed as far as the streams were concerned. "But they don't flow all year. You may be right about the High Rock. I dunno."

Hopalong headed along the trail of the missing cattle and took his time. It was true the farther they managed to travel before they were overtaken and recovered, the farther the cattle must be driven to get them back. On the other hand, the farther they went unmolested, the surer they would be of safety, and safety would lull their suspicions, cause them to grow less watchful.

"There's a place up there," Frank Gillespie offered suddenly, "called Agate. She ain't what a feller would call a town, but she's a place. To one side of the road is the hotel and saloon, to the other side a livery stable with a few old crow-bait cayuses. Feller name of Sourdough runs the livery stable and another, name of Mormon John, runs the saloon.

"Only," Gillespie added, "Mormon John ain't no Mormon. He just talks about Mormon women all the time. Him and Sourdough been fightin' back an' forth for six or seven years. Maybe it's because they ain't nothin' else to do."

"Saloon, eh? Reckon those rustlers will stop there?"

"Might. He's got whiskey there, only it's his own make and mean enough to make a jack rabbit run a grizzly into his hole. Worse than Injun whiskey they used to peddle when I was a kid.

"She's just raw corn whisky that he soups up with a little Jimson weed, but it'll sure get you fightin' and climbin' if you're in a mood for it."

They rode on in silence, each occupied with his thoughts. The moon was floating lower in the sky, and occasionally Hopalong dismounted to study the trail. The cattle tracks were still plain, and he did not like the look of it. There was no sense to this trail. There had to be concealment somewhere. Either that or it was a trap. He said as much and they slowed down, advancing with extreme care. It was useless, for the trail led on into the mountain valleys, occasionally crossing a low saddle, but pushing on and on.

No rustler in his right mind would leave so obvious a trail. Yet this one was being left, and they were free to follow it. That meant one of two things: either a trap up ahead or something unusual in the way of disappearing cattle. Just before moonset the trail petered out.

"No use ridin' now," Hopalong said. "We'll camp here and move on come daybreak."

Morning found them in the saddle once more, but there

was no trail. Swinging wide, one to each side of the dim trail they had followed, they attempted to cut sign, but there was none. The herd they had followed had disappeared without a trace!

There was but one thing to do, Hopalong decided, and that was to turn back until they found the point where the herd had vanished. Seven miles back along the trail they again came upon the tracks of the herd. Yet even here they could not decide at exactly what point the cattle had vanished. Either the herd had dwindled bit by bit into the desert or it had vanished into thin air.

The sand of the desert was not hard-packed and laden with rocks or overgrown with desert brush and cacti; instead it was loose and gray, unbelievably fine for the most part, and in this surface the prints sank and were lost. The slightest shifting wind served to wipe out a track.

Gillespie reined in and stared disgustedly at the desert. "Look there, Hoppy! That's where we rode not over an hour ago, and the tracks are gone! Every durned breeze that can tilt a grass blade starts this sand a-blowin'. That herd walked off into the desert, and from there it might have gone anywhere!"

Hopalong stared through narrowed eyes at the mountains beyond the waste. Probably the cattle had gone over there, but those mountains stretched for seventy or eighty miles to the northward, and there was no telling how far the cattle had been driven. Yet there was a limit, too, and that limit was the distance they would go without dying of thirst.

"You might as well go back, Frank," he said at last. "This will be a mighty long job. You head back to the ranch and tell 'em where I am. Don't tell anybody else. Meanwhile I'll ride on to this place called Agate. Whether I find the trail or not, I'll be in Agate the day after tomorrow. If there's any news, have somebody meet me there with it. I don't think I'll need any help yet, but they might need it back at the ranch."

Frank Gillespie hesitated and swore. "Durn it all, Hoppy, I wanted to be in on the showdown with them rustlers! I've come this far. Still"—he was disgusted—"as you say, they're gonna need me back there. We're mighty short-handed."

After the cowhand had gone, Hopalong sat his horse and studied the situation. The herd might have gone into that desert all right, and it might have only been walked in it a way and then driven back out on the same side. That would stand investigation before crossing the desert into the rough country beyond.

Speaking to the black, he started along the desert's edge. Whether he found the trail or not, he had every idea that the rustlers, or some of them, might stop at Agate, and there was a chance he might get news of them there. In the meantime he would soon know whether the herd had been driven out of the sand again.

This was very rugged country; the timber of the region to the east here thinned out and most of the mountains were bare except for low brush and desert growth. Yet there was plenty of cover, and farther west there was both water and grass in the remote High Rock Canyon country. No matter who was directing the move, whether Jack Bolt or Sim Aragon, they would have a chance of holding the cattle for months in that rough country without being seen.

The tracks of the herd had not emerged from the desert but when the buildings of Agate were in sight, a lone rider came out of the sand and headed towards the town. Hopalong slowed down and took his time. The rider might be somebody he had never seen, and somebody who had not seen him. The livery stable would be the first stop, and then the saloon.

The western saloon was always a clearing house for information. It was much more than a drinking establishment, for it was the center of all male social life. Here trail news was repeated, cattle were discussed as were all the varied topics of interest to western men. The saloon was at once a reception room, a social club, and a source of information. Sooner or later all news came to light around a saloon, and if a man had time and patience he could learn much by simply being around and listening. Hopalong knew this and if the strange rider had been one of the rustlers, he was sure he would find out before he had been long in Agate.

The livery stable was a rambling red-painted barn with a high-peaked roof over the center part and almost flat roofs over the two wings. There was an office with two lighted windows beside the big door of the stable, and the door was open. In the rectangle of lantern light a lean, hard-faced oldster sat, smoking a pipe. From what Gillespie had said, Cassidy knew that this was Sourdough. He looked up balefully as Hopalong swung down.

"Got an empty stall? And some corn?"

The old man took his pipe from his teeth. "Corn?" He was incredulous. "You gonna feed corn to that cayuse?"

"That cayuse is a mighty fine horse," Hopalong said calmly, "and any horse I ride gets the best."

The old man pointed with his pipe stem. "Third stall. Corn is in the feed bin. Watch out for that bay—he kicks mighty wicked."

When Hopalong had stripped the saddle from the black he fed it an ample supply of corn, then strolled outside, shoving back his black wide-brimmed hat. The lamplight gleamed on his snowy hair.

Neither man spoke. The night was very still. Far out over the desert a coyote yapped in a shrill, complaining voice, and across the street at the saloon there was a shout of laughter, then the bang of a bottle on the bar. The night air was cool, and there was a vast spread of stars that looked amazingly bright and near. The livery had the good smells of a horse barn, of stored hay and feed, of horses and sweaty leather. In the distance the serrated ridge of mountains drew a ragged black line.

Darkness had come, and in the shadow of his hat the old man's face could not be seen. Only the glow of his pipe was visible. Beyond him the town's street, which was also the trail, showed white against the darker earth. Two cabins were lighted, but all other buildings loomed dark and sullen except for the saloon.

"Mighty restful," Hopalong suggested, squatting on his heels. "Does a man good to relax once in a while."

Sourdough grunted, drawing on his pipe. It seemed to have gone out, and he struck a match, then sucked to get it going better.

"See many riders through here?" Hopalong asked.

The old man merely grunted again, but made no further reply. Hopalong decided to use strategy. "Of course," he said, "you can't expect much in a place like this. Out of the way, like it is. A man might come through here once a week or ten days. I don't see how you keep alive."

"We do all right."

Encouraged, Hopalong shook his head. "Beats me how you do it. There aren't enough people. I'd bet there ain't five men in that saloon right now. And I'll bet all of them are from right here in town."

Sourdough glared at him through the darkness. "A lot you know!" he scoffed. "There's eight men over there right now, and only three of 'em are from right here!"

"Three?" Hopalong grinned. "You mean to say five strangers are in town at once?"

Sourdough bristled. "I didn't say nothin' about strangers. These here hombres ain't strangers. They just don't live right here in town. Peter Aragon has him a ranch back in the hills somewheres, and two of them fellers ride for him. What the others do I wouldn't say."

Hopalong rubbed his chin thoughtfully. Pete Aragon was one of the men in the saloon, and the others were his friends. The chances were these men were driving the herd and had come to town for a drink or two, after which they would return to the stolen cattle. It was doubtful that more than three men had been left behind as guards.

Jack Bolt had only six men of his own and the Aragon outfit numbered seven all told, which meant thirteen men at least were available. Some of these would be needed on the home ranch and some would be left in the hills to scout for Connors. Eight was probably a good guess at the number with the herd, and five were here in Agate.

Watching the lights of the saloon, he studied the situation with care. He hesitated to enter the saloon, yet knew that some of them had probably heard his horse when he arrived and if he did not come in they would be suspicious.

Sourdough knocked out his pipe, then stoked it with fresh tobacco. Hopalong gave him a sidelong glance, wondering how much he could get out of the old man. He knew the method of obtaining information now at least.

"A long time ago," he said, "I knew a man named Tedrue. He was a good friend to a fellow in my outfit. That Tedrue was a woodsman and a hunter as well as a rider. He told me about a valley over west of here where there was plenty of grass and water, but from the look of this country he must've been mistaken. I'd say there wasn't a drop of water in miles of that country."

Sourdough took his pipe from his mouth. "And you'd be wrong!" he said flatly. "I knowed that there Tedrue, and he knowed this here country most as well as I do! He was sure a-tellin' of the truth!"

"Aw!" Cassidy protested. "Just look around. Black sand and bare hills. Not a sign of water. I'd bet you'd have to go nearly to the coast before you'd find water."

"Huh!" The old man grunted his disgust. "Sure wouldn't! I could name you fifty water holes, and even some lakes over thataway!" He drew deep and his pipe glowed. Somebody laughed loud in the saloon. The old man pointed towards a distant peak. "There's a water hole at the foot of that peak. The country west of here has plenty of hot springs, too.

"Why, there's one section over there a man has to walk mighty easy or he'll go through. The whole surface of the ground is underlaid by one big hot spring, boilin' water that'll take the hide right off a man if he should fall into it!

"There's water in High Rock all right, and in Little High Rock. Summit Lake is one of the prettiest lakes you ever laid eyes on. A mite farther west is the Massacre Lakes—mostly dry this time of year, though. Injun country, that is, and plenty of Modocs still around. Jesse Applegate went through there, and so did Lassen. There's lost mines, too. Me, I prospected all over that country. Tedrue, he come through there as a boy, and what he told was the truth, believe you me."

Hopalong got to his feet. "Well, I could be wrong," he said, "and it sure is good to find a man that knows the country. I like to talk to an hombre who knows what he's talkin' about. I reckon I'll have a look around that saloon."

Somewhat mollified by Hopalong's flattery, Sourdough looked up at him. "You be mighty careful in yonder," he said. "Some of that bunch is plumb salty, and Pete Aragon ain't the worst of them!"

CHAPTER 7

Swift Gunplay

Slowly Hopalong walked across the street and opened the door of the saloon. At once faces turned towards him. Hard-featured faces of roughly dressed men, and all were armed, several wearing two guns. Head and shoulders above them stood Mormon John, a huge black-bearded man with thick eyebrows. The gaze of this towering giant met that of Hopalong over the crowd, and Cassidy was sure he saw a glint of sudden interest in the big man's eyes. What the others were thinking Hopalong could not guess. He walked to the bar and slowly looked around the room.

Long and low-ceilinged, it was only a third as wide as its length, and on the side opposite the door was a long bar. Hopalong nodded to Mormon John. "Howdy! I take it you're Mormon John?"

"You got it right, stranger. Somethin' for you?"

"Not right now," Hopalong said. "Just passing by and thought I'd drop in. I was talking to your friend Sourdough."

"My friend?" Mormon John exploded. "That old rawhider? That son of a sheepherder a friend of mine? You heard wrong, stranger, if you heard that."

"That right?" Hopalong looked amazed. "Well, now, what do you know about that? He didn't say anything bad about you, mister."

A heavy-faced man standing nearer to Hopalong than the others stared hard at Cassidy. "Where've I seen you before?" he demanded.

Hopalong looked the man over carefully. The face was unfamiliar, but the type was not. "Why, I don't reckon you have," he said quietly. "I know you don't look like anything *I've* ever seen before."

Somebody chuckled a little, and the man's face darkened. He straightened a little from the bar. "Too many of you grub-line riders around here," he said. "Why don't you drift north and git clear out of the country?"

Hopalong considered the question gravely. "I like it here," he said at last. "Fact is, I'm figuring on starting my own outfit. I am riding west right now and figure to find a place over in the High Rock country."

The hands holding drinks froze in position. He was looking down at the bar, but sensed all eyes were upon him.

"That there's a bad area." The new speaker was a narrow-faced man with black eyes. There was an ugly scar on his right cheek that looked as if it had been torn by claws. "Good country to stay shut of."

Hopalong shrugged. "Could be, but I like a place without fences and I hear there's both grass and water over there, and land for the taking."

One by one the men downed their drinks. The man with the scar on his face turned to one of those beside him. "Reckon we better go, Vila."

"Sure, Pete."

Vila turned and walked to the door, pausing there. Pete

had not moved, yet from some unseen gesture one of the men nearest him straightened, placed his glass on the bar, walked across to the window, and stopped there with his back to it.

The big man who had started hunting trouble spoke softly. "You stay out of that High Rock country. Folks over thataway don't cotton to strangers."

Hopalong Cassidy said nothing at all. He knew the value of suspense, of waiting. He also knew his own nerves, and now he stood very still and let his eyes go from one face to another. Slowly the seconds passed, and the tension grew. Somebody swallowed and the sound was plain to them all. Then Vila shifted his feet slightly. Hopalong's eyes moved on to Pete Aragon and stopped there. Pete was the boss—and was less charged with killing tension than Vila.

"That right?" Hopalong said gently. "Now that's too bad, isn't it?"

Hopalong was not looking for trouble. He had wanted information and he had wanted to see these men, for the more of them he knew by sight, the better off he would be. Furthermore, if anything did begin, he wanted them to begin it.

"Yeah," he continued, "that is too bad. It would be a nice country to locate in, but me, I'm a peace-loving man." He pulled his hat down on his head. As he started to turn from the bar he perceived, by the sudden stiffening of the watchers, that he was not going to get away without trouble. Some signal had evidently passed from Pete Aragon which he had overlooked, yet he continued his turn and brought his foot down hard on the big man's toe. The man cried out and jumped back. Instantly Hopalong grabbed iron.

His move had been abrupt and unexpected, and although they had planned to take him, Aragon's men were caught by surprise. Hopalong's seeming unawareness of the situation had put them off guard. Moreover, they had covered the doors and windows through which he might escape, but there was nobody behind him. Hopalong's sudden move put the big man between him and the others, and now he held, by virtue of that flashing draw, two six-guns.

"Move back." He indicated the big fellow. "You fall back with your partners. You, Pete, tell your boys not to start anything they can't finish. The first person I nail will be you."

Vila was glaring, his tongue touching his lips. This was the man to watch; Hopalong Cassidy had seen gunmen too many times not to realize that the Mexican was dangerous. He was tightly strung and had that kind of nervous energy that builds up to an explosive pitch.

Pete Aragon was worried. He knew Vila, and knew the Mexican was quite capable of attempting a draw even when covered—if the slightest chance offered itself. "No use to get upset," Pete said carefully. "We just mentioned that was bad country up there. We weren't huntin' trouble."

"Take it easy, then," Hopalong replied easily. "I'm driftin'. If you get trouble, it will be because you start it." He let his eyes wander over the faces of the watching men and then swung his back to the door and in three steps felt the edge of the door against his shoulder. Nobody had moved.

"Better drift on out of the country," Pete suggested quietly. "It ain't healthy around here for gunslingers."

Hopalong's cold features relaxed in an ironic smile. "No? Then suppose you boys take that advice. You drift—I'm stickin'. In fact, I may take a job ridin' for the 3TL."

Aragon stiffened, and Vila's clawlike fingers tensed. Both men glared at him. Holstering a gun, Hopalong dropped his left hand to the doorknob, and turning it, he stepped out into the night. Crossing to the stable, he stepped quickly into the darkness. His horse was unsaddled and needed rest. It would take minutes to saddle it, and by that time they could be out and have all trails covered. He would have to shoot his way through. The best and safest place was right here. He turned, looking around for the old miner.

Sourdough's dry voice came out of the darkness. "Surprised," he said. "I never figured you'd get back here alive. Figured that horse of Dan Keating's would be left here for me."

"You know that horse?"

"Knowed Keating hisself. Mighty fine man. Always figured I'd like to get my sights on the hombre what shot him."

"Don't blame me for that," Cassidy said shortly. "I got this horse in Tascotal to replace my own."

"Yeah," Sourdough said, "I guessed as much. You couldn't get a hand on him unless Letsinger figured you to be all right." He stared across the street as the door opened and men poured into the street. "What now?"

"I'm crawling into the hay in your loft," Hopalong said. "I don't feel like running." So saying, he swung and went up the ladder. In an instant he was lost in darkness. Sourdough struck a match and lighted up his pipe, then returned to the worn chair by the door.

Pete Aragon's voice sounded suddenly, and Hopalong heard his every word. "Sourdough? You see an hombre come out here a minute ago?"

"Reckon somebody did come out. I was back inside gettin' matches, but I heard the door close."

"You didn't see anybody in the street? Or on the trail?"

"Yeah, a while back I did. Feller went into the saloon yonder. Anybody," he added truthfully, "comin' into the stable would've had to pass right by me. This hombre might have left his cayuse outside of town. He might be headed back thataway." Which, he reflected, was nothing less than true. Hopalong could have left his horse outside of town. The fact that he had not was quite another thing.

Aragon turned and spoke rapidly to two of his men. Both mounted and rode rapidly down the trail. Sourdough puffed contentedly at his pipe. The truth, Hoppy decided, could be a very pliable thing.

After a while the rest of them saddled up and left town, and Hopalong relaxed contentedly into the hay. It smelled fresh and good. He was very tired.

It was daylight when he awakened to see Sourdough bending over him. "Fixed you some grub," the old man said. "Better eat and get. This here town ain't safe for you."

Hopalong got quickly to his feet and brushed off the hay. Descending the ladder, he walked into the old man's living quarters. He grinned widely when he saw the eggs and ham. Quickly he washed up and combed his hair, then drew up a chair and started in. Sourdough chuckled when he saw him eat.

"Now that's the way a man should eat! I like to see a real appetite, not one of these here picky kind of fellers who muddle over their grub and never eat up. Never seen a cowhand nor any kind of workin' or fightin' man who ever left grub on his plate!"

Hopalong chuckled. "You're right, old-timer. Do I smell hot cakes?"

"You just wait! I got a stack comin' up for you."

Hopalong glanced out of the window. Mormon John was standing on his steps, looking across the street. There was nobody else in sight. The tracks of the horses could be plainly seen from where he sat, and all were going out of town, none coming back.

Mormon John looked curiously up the street towards the trail out of town. He scowled, then turned and walked back inside. Hopalong considered the action and looked up. Casually he asked, "I recall a couple of buildings between here and the edge of town. Is there anyone living over there?"

"Uh-uh. Just a couple of empty shacks and the old Gold Strike Saloon. Ain't been anybody in 'em for years."

Watching the saloon, Cassidy saw Mormon John come outside again. Obviously the big man was curious and trying to conceal his curiosity. He came out now and began sweeping the porch before the saloon, pausing from time to time to look around, but his attention centered itself on the trail towards the west or something in that direction.

Sourdough brought the pot and filled Hopalong's cup once more. He seemed oblivious of Hopalong's interest in what was happening outside. After a minute or so Hopalong got up, stretched, and changed his seat. He tried the fresh cup of coffee. From the new position he had taken he could see down the trail. The faded sign on the Gold Strike indicated that building. In the rear corner there was a window. Could Mormon John have seen something in that window?

As he sipped coffee Hopalong listened to the idle rambling of Sourdough's conversation. Once started, the old man was ready enough to talk, and his talking concerned the trail west and the country that lay out thataway, as he phrased it.

"Applegate done started that trail," Sourdough advised, "and Pete Lassen used part of it on his own cutoff. Folks in them days was in a powerful hurry to get rich. They figured once they was in Californy they would have no trouble pickin' up plenty of gold, so when that Humboldt Trail swung south they didn't like it much.

"Them that tackled the Applegate and Lassen routes, they

cussed the livin' daylights out of both men for startin' it. Mighty scarce grass and less water, unless you knowed exactly where to look, and them days nobody knowed but the Injuns. But what Injuns they was wasn't friendly.

"Rabbit Hole Springs they found because of rabbit tracks. Why, even the Humboldt didn't have much water in it. There was a young feller named Clemens workin' on a paper down in Virginny City who says a feller could tire himself jumpin' back and forth across the river and then drink it dry when he got himself thirsty.

"Lots of hot springs over west. Lassen got hisself killed over there, huntin' silver. Clapper Crick's right back up thataway. Clapper was killed with Lassen. Maybe by Injuns, maybe by a partner. Nobody ever rightly knowed. North of there you'll find water at Soldier Meadows, and there's plenty of water and grass up Mud Lake Valley."

He paused for breath, and Hopalong finished the last of his coffee, only lukewarm now. He stretched his muscles.

"Reckon I'll leave now, Sourdough," he said. "Wish you'd go to the stable and saddle up for me. I've got a little job to do first."

The old man looked at him quickly, struck by some tone in Hopalong's voice. "Somebody stayed behind." Cassidy nodded. "There's a man in that old saloon. I'd lay a month's wages on it."

He waited after the old man went out, watching the saloon. Then he went swiftly to the back of the livery stable and out a door into the corrals. For an instant he stood there, letting his eyes grow accustomed to the glare of the bright morning sun. It was pleasant just to stand there and feel the warmth and brightness, to smell the rich barnyard smells, and over them the faint yet tangible odor of the sage-clad hills. Then he crossed to the corral fence and slid between the bars.

He stood now at the corner of the barn. Removing his hat, he peered around the edge, studying the situation.

The nearest house was some thirty feet away across a gravel alleyway. From where he stood only a corner of the saloon could be seen, and the merest edge of the saloon window. The unseen gunman's only chance of seeing him would be if he was pressed tightly against that edge of the window, and in any event he would have no chance to fire. Hopalong pulled his hat on, took a step back, then launched himself in a swift run to the back wall of the house. He drew up and stood still, listening.

There was no sound. The boards of the old house were brown with age and they smelled of the heat. Edging along behind the building, he peered through a window that allowed him to see through the empty house and watch the front of the saloon. As he watched he saw a shadow slip by a window opposite to his. He had been right, then. Someone had been left behind in case he had hidden in the town.

On tiptoe, placing each foot down gently, Hopalong worked his way to the corner of the building. The neighboring house, which was the last in town, jutted at least ten feet farther towards the road than his present hiding place. To cross to its shelter he would have to allow himself in full view of the saloon for at least three steps. Time enough to drop him if the watcher was ready.

Listening, Hopalong Cassidy heard a horse walking in the gravel in front of the livery stable. Evidently Sourdough had led the black outside for water. That would certainly attract the watcher's eyes. In three quick steps Hopalong made the back of the neighboring house, but even as he leaped behind it, a gun bellowed and he heard the angry thud of a bullet!

Swinging around the corner of the house, he dropped flat at its corner and edged forward. The Gold Strike's swing doors had been enclosed inside the heavy outer doors put up when the saloon was closed. Now the outer door stood partly open, and Hopalong thought he saw the blackness of a boot. He lifted his pistol and took a snap shot past the corner.

Instantly a gun boomed and a heavy slug ripped through the corner of the house just inches over his head, showering him with splinters. Another shot came through higher, and then one lower that almost nicked him! Jerking back, he lay still, waiting. His shot must have been wasted. Whoever the watcher was, he was using a rifle—probably, by the sound, a Spencer.

He groaned suddenly, then again, and softer in tone. The air was still, and he was sure the sound would reach the gunman. Whether he would be taken in by the ruse was quite another thing, but it was worth trying. Hopalong waited while a man might have counted ten and then moaned softly, as if in pain.

There was no sound within the saloon. The air was warm and very still. A door slammed down the street; then all was silent once more. A lizard eased itself from under the porch and peered, bright-eyed and curious, at Hopalong. He waited, heard a faint creak of boards from within the saloon, then no other sound.

A hat appeared, and he waited. The hat was withdrawn and there were sounds of movement within the saloon. Drawing back, Hopalong tiptoed around the house and peered from the back corner. The door was partly open now, as if the gunman were looking towards the corner at which he had fired. Unexpectedly, the man emerged. It was Vila.

Gun in hand, but a pistol this time, for close work, the desperado stepped off the porch into the street. Instantly Hopalong stepped into the open.

"Vila!" he shouted. "Drop it!"

The outlaw whirled as if touched by a spark, and dropping into a half-crouch, he fired. Despite the speed of his turn, the bullet flicked dangerously near Hopalong's cheek. Cassidy thumbed the hammer of his gun. The outlaw sprang back, his pistol sliding from his fingers, a red gash across the back of his hand. With his left he grabbed for his other gun, but a bullet cut between belt and gun butt and he jerked his hand clear, blood dripping from a thumb knuckle. Slowly he lifted his hands.

"That's better," Hopalong said quietly, "much better. My advice then is to get out of this country, and fast!"

"Not me!" Vila's face was vicious. "I'll kill you for this."

CHAPTER 8

Dangerous Country

$\mathbf{I}$n some secret place among the canyons west of the desert the stolen herds would be held, and it was to that country now that Hopalong Cassidy turned the palouse. Hopalong allowed the horse to set its own gait, and despite the heat of the day, they moved swiftly.

Now there was a definite trail, and studying the tracks of the various horses, Hopalong picked out, one by one, the hoofprints of each. Soon some of them might turn off, and he wanted to know who he was following. Without doubt one of the leaders would be Pete Aragon—which he hoped to discover before long, for Aragon was one man of whom he wished to keep track. The horse on the left front was peculiarly gaited; the toes of the hoofs pointing out somewhat, the buttresses inward. Another of the group had bar shoes. Studying the tracks as they moved along proved other things to Hopalong. One of the horses kept fighting the bit. More often than any of the others it broke the formation in which they rode and had to be forced back alongside his mate.

The trail now left the greasewood-covered sandhills and emerged upon the sand of the desert itself. Hopalong drew up and studied the situation carefully. Although the desert gave every appearance of openness, there was actually room to conceal an army if it was properly disposed. Yet he knew that to investigate every hummock, every hill, would take much too long. He would have to keep his eyes open and gamble.

Several times he saw dust ahead of him, but at no time did he see the riders. They were heading for a canyon that seemed to cut deep into the range of mountains that lay ahead. From what Sourdough had said, in this direction might lie the Pahute Meadows, and if so, it offered a possible route through and over the mountains into the arm of the desert that lay beyond them, and at the base of Pahute Peak there was water. Somewhere in the vicinity would be Clapper Creek.

Sweat coursed down his face and thick dust lifted and settled over him and over the black shining coat of the palouse. He pulled his hat brim lower and let his eyes seek out every bit of available cover as he came towards it, ever alert for movement, the glisten of sun on a rifle barrel, or any other indication that an enemy was near. Whether they would trust only to Vila he did not know. In any event, he must push on.

The mountains were now a solid wall before him, and their blackness changed and showed streaks of brown and gray, and there was considerable growth on their rugged slopes. The green of Pahute Meadows showed, and Hopalong slowed the palouse despite the horse's anxious tuggings at the bit.

The black knew there was water ahead, and grass. Of the men with rifles who rode before him he knew nothing. Yet Hopalong saw that the man with the slue-gaited horse had fallen back and another ridden ahead. The chances were that Pete was riding ahead and on the right, for he was the only one who held to his position. Hopalong studied the track in particular.

When he came to the meadows they were deserted, yet here there was green grass, and Hopalong swung down. After watering the palouse he picketed the horse, and while it cropped at the rich green grass he walked about. His search was soon rewarded, for he stumbled upon the tracks of the cattle almost at once. Here the group led by Pete Aragon had fallen in with the trail of the cattle he had followed earlier, proving his gamble—that some of the riders would leave the herd for a drink in Agate—had paid off.

After thirty minutes Hopalong tightened his girth and swung back into the saddle. Now the canyon narrowed and the rocky walls towered above him. There were trees here and there, and more brush. The cattle had been several hours ahead of the other riders at this point, but the riders would move faster and should soon overtake the herd.

It was not enough to find them. Not enough even to have recovered the herd, if that was possible. What he wanted most was to find where the cattle were being taken—hence, where the others had gone before. Comradeships of the cattle trails were often thicker than blood itself, and Hopalong liked Gibson. Moreover, the man was a part of the memories he loved best, of the old days of the Bar 20. And these men had attacked and tried to kill his friend Red Connors.

The desert sun blistered the flat, reflecting rocks, and in the canyon it was like an oven. Hopalong's shirt turned dark with sweat, and his horse walked slower, feeling the heat. The way widened at last and the tracks of the cattle were plain, leading onward and over a flat, high plateau. Here the air was clear, and the heat seemed less. Hopalong's eyes and ears were alert now, for he knew that soon he should be coming up to the moving herd.

Then suddenly the world broke off before him; the plateau

ended and slid off in a series of ledges, making in all a gigantic declivity, an enormous stair that led down by devious trails to a meadow far below. Hopalong mopped his face and studied the rocky descent with careful eyes. If a man was shot here he could roll or fall a long way, and every foot of the trail now was filled with increasing danger. Then he spoke to the horse and moved on. Ears pricked up, the palouse chose his own path, following the trail of the cattle and the riders.

Suddenly, far below, Hopalong saw a moving black dot. Instantly he drew up. After a moment he saw that one moving thing was followed by others. The herd!

There was a man riding point, then the cattle flanked and followed by riders. Studying the situation, he saw nothing in it to like. From here on much of his trail would keep him hopelessly in the open, and having just traversed that trail, nobody would know it better than Aragon and his riders. As Vila had not caught up to them, they might guess that something had happened to him. If there were some of the Jack Bolt hands with the cattle, they would know about Cassidy and would surely tell Aragon.

To descend that steep trail now would be to ask for trouble. Most of it led over bare rock faces, and the only possible shelter was from occasional boulders, which could just as easily offer an ambush by one of the riders he was following. Regretfully, Hopalong turned the black towards a cluster of rocks near the foot of the first ledge.

Swinging down, he stripped the saddle from the palouse and then, getting a handful of dry grass, he rubbed the big horse down. The palouse stood quietly, gratefully accepting his attentions.

"That boss of yours," Hopalong said, "knew how to care for a horse. I can tell by the way you act, old-timer. Only a horse that's been treated right would stand as quietly as you do."

He sponged out the horse's mouth with some water from his canteen, and only then did he take a drink himself. Afterwards he poured some water in his hat and let the horse drink it. Then he seated himself in the shade of a boulder and waited, studying with his glasses the country that lay before him.

Going down that mountain in the dark would be no picnic. Moreover, it was probable the tracks would give out on those ledges. The droppings of the cattle might help, but they would leave no hoofprints on those flat rocks.

The slow afternoon drew on, and the sun stared him in the face. Then shadows began to gather on the eastern side of the mountains. The canyons filled with darkness, brimful and mysterious in the late afternoon, and then there was the blue stillness of twilight. He mounted, and the horse walked on, eager to be moving. The evening air smelled of sage and the faint memory of the cattle that had passed. The palouse found a way down to the next long ledge and descended. Here Hopalong had to scout for a way off the flat, and it was full dark before he found it—a thin, winding trail among boulders and then across the bald, open face of the mountain.

The moon came up, and its light changed the landscape below him—an eerie greenish glow lay over the bald peaks and the great shoulders of rock. They loomed up, deathly still and lonely as he wove his way down among them until at last he smelled the good fresh smell of green grass and the dampness of land overgrown. Suddenly his nostrils detected something else. He drew up, head forward, sniffing the night. The smell brought no recognition to his mind, only a faintly disturbing sense. After a minute he spoke to the horse and started on. A hoof clicked on stone, and the stone tumbled down the steep path before him, a fall that ended in a splash. At the same time the horse stopped abruptly, shying from something ahead.

As he swung down, Hopalong's boot sounded hollowly on the rock, and he hesitated, peering around. And then it came to him! He smelled steam.

Steam!

He picked up a rock and tossed it down the hill. It chunked into water with a thick gulp, and taking a step forward, he heard again that hollowness under his feet. At the same instant something cracked and rock gave way under him!

He sprang, scrambled wildly over the crumbling rock, and managed to get a hand on a stirrup as the palouse swung around. When he felt solid ground under his feet he stopped, sweat breaking out on his face. He knew then what had happened. He had almost fallen into a hot spring! Sourdough had told him of those boiling springs that lay in this country, and how in places they underlay large areas. Once a heavy wagon had broken through the crust, and pioneers had boiled eggs in the water and cooked fish in it.

"We'll camp right here, boy," he said quietly. "No sense in taking any chances."

With the first gray of dawn he was up, and what he saw made his eyes glint with anger. The crust had been carefully broken through—broken right across the trail so that a rider could scarcely avoid going right into it! It was a deadly trap, which he had escaped only by the accident of a splashing stone and the good sense of his horse. Yet it was a warning of what he might expect from the men he was following. They would hesitate at nothing to stop him. A step farther last night, or less luck in escaping the crumbling rock, and he might have been horribly burned or even boiled alive.

. . .

Back at the headquarters of the 8 Boxed H, Jack Bolt was nervously pacing the floor. The news that Hopalong Cassidy, as well as Connors, was in the vicinity worried him. This might be too good to last, and with men of that type coming into the country, it began to look as if it had reached the end. The only thing was to complete the cleanup they had planned and then sit tight.

He had talked with Grat, and had heard Sim Aragon's statement that he would take care of Cassidy. Yet Bolt was too shrewd to put all his eggs in one basket, especially when those eggs depended on the outwitting and killing of a man as salty and gun-slick as Hopalong Cassidy. Nothing had been seen of Cassidy, and that worried him even more. Nor of Connors. But the chances were great that Connors was dead. Yet Connors dead might be a greater damage than alive, for he might be a rallying point for all of the old Bar 20 crowd.

Something had to be done, and whatever it was, it had to be done fast. Abel Garson drifted into the ranch yard just at that time. Garson was a man of no importance. He was a hanger-on and a loafer, a man who drank but never was drunk, who lived by knowing things and telling the right people what he knew. He also rustled a few cows from time to time, and one way and another kept soul and body together. Now he dropped from his saddle and slouched towards Bolt.

Bolt stopped, chewed a moment, then spat. "What's on your mind?" he demanded, resting his sharp eyes on Garson.

The man took his cigarette from his mouth. "Just come from Tascotal. There's talk goin' around, Jack. Folks saw Sim

Aragon with some of your boys yesterday. That Joe Gamble of the 3F. He's been askin' questions around."

Bolt swore viciously. "I told that fool Grat not to let Bones come into town with Sim!" he declared. "Where's Gamble now?"

Garson shrugged. "Slipped out of town. He was askin' about Red Connors, too, and askin' various folks if they had lost cows."

"I was afraid of that." Bolt went into his pocket and came out with ten dollars. "Stick that in your kick, Abel. Anything you hear, let me know."

Garson nodded. "Trouble last night up at Agate. Pete Aragon and some of his boys had a run-in with a white-headed feller carrying a plated pair of Colts. He backed 'em down. Vila rode in this mornin' to see the Doc—he had a bad hand. Tim and Pod was talkin' some. This same white-headed gent run Pod off the 3TL. Pod is rantin' around that he'll kill him. Says he's that Hopalong Cassidy, from down Texas way."

"He is." Jack Bolt had been the first person Pod had told. Fury mounted within him. Aragon at Agate! When would they learn to play it safe and smart? They should never have left the cattle. Now Vila was wounded and Pod swearing vengeance. This last item held his interest. If Hopalong was killed now, it would be very easy to place the blame on Pod, angry because he had been fired. Nevertheless, even if that was accomplished, things were piling up. Too many things were going wrong, and they had started with the arrival of Red Connors in the country.

"Go back to town," Bolt said, "and talk it around that you heard Pod had a run-in with Cassidy. And keep your ears open. I want to know everything that 3TL outfit does."

It might be time to go all out. He didn't want it that way,

but this might be the time. Kill Cassidy, Connors, and Gamble —out of town, if possible, and make a grand cleanup on the cattle, then sit tight and see what happened.

High on the slope of Copper Mountain, Red Connors was feeling better. Plenty to eat and drink, the high, pure air, and rest had done marvels for him. His wound was healing rapidly, and he was growing restless with inactivity. Somewhere down below, Hopalong was busy and might be needing him. There was still plenty of grub and his horse was in fine shape, but Red was growing restless. Moreover, he had been shot at too often without a chance to return the courtesy.

"That Hoppy!" he growled half-aloud. "He's stealin' all the fun!"

Sitting at the mouth of the cave with the glass in his hand, he could study the terrain below him by picking holes in the green belt of the trees that surrounded the cave entrance. He was studying this countryside when he saw a rider on a tobiano riding along a trail some distance off. The man was moving slowly and studying the country. This rider was Joe Gamble, far off his own grounds and trying to pick up some sign of either Connors or the stolen cattle. Yet the distance was too great for Red to see the 3F brand on the horse Gamble was riding.

Watching the rider, Red decided that he had without doubt lost the trail. "Now that there's a positive shame," Red muttered to his horse. "That hombre ain't goin' to find me, an' if he don't, I miss out on what might be a good scrap. Maybe I'd better lend him a hand."

Getting his gear, Red saddled the horse and then, with his

rifle in hand, he mounted up. Once under cover of the trees, he worked his way through the timber until he came upon the rider's trail. He was just starting down it when he saw Gamble returning and immediately recognized both the man and the brand. Stepping from the brush, he held up a hand.

"Red Connors!" Gamble grinned. "Sure and I was huntin' you."

"What's happenin' below? Hoppy around?"

"He's off somewhere, an' busy. I reckon he hit a hot trail and follered it."

Joe tugged a bag of tobacco from his pocket and while they smoked, he brought Red Connors up to date on the situation as he knew it, including the rumors of the fight at Agate and the arrival of Vila with one hand deeply grazed by a bullet and a thumb knuckle skinned to the bone.

"That sounds like Hoppy. He's no hand to kill a man unless he's forced to it. Howsoever, from what I've heard of that Vila, I wished he had done the job on him."

Gamble agreed. "He's all bad. Not a good point in the man, and plenty of meanness an' trouble down his back trail. Even outlaws can't get along with him."

Connors was studying the situation. "The cattle I follered," he said, "came east, but that don't mean all of 'em have. Fact is, I was some puzzled that I found no old tracks along the way. The herd I was tailin' seemed to be blazin' a trail."

"Could be," Gamble agreed. "It wouldn't be easy to get cattle out of the country goin' east. Not as a regular thing. Jack Bolt would know that, an' so would the Aragons. West of here —well, you can ride that country for days and never see a man nor a cow. Wild horses in there, lots of antelope and coyotes, and nothing much else. If they wanted to drive west they could probably find a market in Oregon. Lots of folks settlin' up that way, but most of those with cows are startin' dairy stock. A man might do purty well with a herd of beef."

"Sure." Red nodded thoughtfully and then made a shrewd guess. "Or maybe he's buildin' his own spread in Oregon or California. Why not? If he never sold anythin' off at all, in a few years the increase would give him a good-sized herd marked with his own brand an' nothin' to worry about.

"I've often figured that rustlers was mighty dumb for not thinkin' of that. Not sellin' the stolen cattle at all, only the steers. Keep the breedin' stock an' build a herd that has no burned-over brands in it."

"Could be done," Gamble agreed. "But you know how rustlers are. They aren't tryin' to get rich, only to get themselves a stake for a big blowout somewheres, or a few months of loafin'. That's the Aragons all over. Jack Bolt, now, he's the cagey one. That hombre is smart, and what he don't know about that sort of thing ain't been written yet. At least, that's the way I figure it.

"Nobody's ever had him tabbed for a rustler. That's one reason I say he's smart. Seein' Bones with Sim Aragon got me to thinkin', an' their reaction to the fact that Cassidy was in the country puzzled me. Then I started puttin' two and two together and she began to add up. Nothin' big, you understand, but lots of little things. Grat's killin' a while back, 8 Boxed H riders seen in odd places—lots of small things that begin to make sense only if you take Bolt and his outfit for cattle thieves."

Red Connors had been thinking on his own hook while following the trend of Gamble's talk. "Hoppy wouldn't take off on no goose chase," he said thoughtfully. "If he started somewhere, it was because he'd been readin' sign. That hombre don't make many mistakes, believe me."

"You fit to ride?" Gamble asked cautiously.

"Fit?" Red bristled. "Sure I'm fit! Been sittin' here frettin' all day."

"Then let's head west. That bunch Cassidy is follerin' are right salty. He may need help."

"It'll be them that needs the help!" Red said emphatically. "But that's no reason we shouldn't ride. No use lettin' him have all the fun. I got a score to settle with that bunch myself. They ran me all over these hills an' just because I run out of cartridges. That Pod Griffin—he must have been the one who stripped my shells."

Sided by Joe Gamble, Red Connors started down the mountain. An unholy joy mounted within him. Just let them try and run him now! With his beloved Winchester and plenty of ammunition he would make them hunt their holes fast! This Gamble seemed a good man. Together they could make a fight of it with anything they encountered, whether it was a rustling gang or a bunch of Modocs on the warpath.

Hopalong had been in Agate, so that was the place to pick up his sign. Their horses' hoofs beat hard on the trail, then softened as they ran through a belt of sand. They rode hard and fast, going by way of Tascotal.

"Reckon we better avoid the town?" Gamble wondered.

"Not on your life!" Connors barked back. "This bunch is hunting trouble! We'll ride right into town, have a drink, and then breeze on through. If anybody wants action, just let them start it!"

Gamble chuckled. "You sound plumb riled, Red. I reckon it must have gone hard with you to let those hombres run you."

"It did," Connors said, "and somebody's goin' to pay for it, too."

CHAPTER 9

Red's "Calling Card"

$\mathbf{H}$ours later they rode into Tascotal. Their horses were weary now and they moved slowly. Red Connors studied the street with hard eyes, taking in the brands of the horses as they pushed into town and swung down at the hitch rack near the bank.

"Don't see any of Bolt's stock," Gamble said, "nor any of the Aragon horses, although they might be ridin' almost anything."

A man walked from the saloon and leaned against the awning post, staring hard at them. Abel Garson was alive with curiosity. Red Connors and Joe Gamble together, and looking like trouble! This would be news for Bolt! And news that, no matter how he liked it, would still pay off. Garson idled on the street, smoking and watching.

"We'll eat," Connors suggested finally, "and then head out and locate Hoppy. I reckon we better ride for that place called Agate. You know the way?"

Gamble nodded, his eyes straying toward Garson. He frowned thoughtfully. He knew nothing good about the man, but little that was bad. Abel Garson was, so far as he knew, merely useless. Yet he was aware of some guarded watchfulness in the man, and made a vow to keep an eye open. They ate then, and from time to time Gamble looked out of the window. Garson had not moved. Yet a few minutes later when he glanced out, the loafer was gone. Still, there was no reason to be excited. So far as Gamble knew, the man had no connection with Bolt or any with Aragon.

Leaving town on the road to Agate, Gamble noted fresh tracks. The trail to the 8 Boxed H turned off from this road. If Garson was a messenger to Bolt, he would be turning off soon. Gamble dropped off his horse and studied the tracks, easily visible in the slanting light of late afternoon.

"Fresh," he said. "Made since that wind went down, which was maybe an hour ago. In this soft sand they'd be almost or entirely wiped out by now if they had been made earlier."

"You see anybody leave?" Connors asked.

"No, but a no-good loafer named Garson was hangin' around. He was gone before we left the restaurant."

Red Connors studied the country ahead. "Know another trail to Agate?"

"Sure, but it's some longer."

"Let's try it, and ride careful." They rode on in silence, and Red chewed thoughtfully. Suddenly he turned his head. "We far from the 8 Boxed H?"

"Three, four miles. There's a horse trail turns off near that pinnacle up ahead." Gamble looked at Red curiously. "What's on your mind?"

Red grinned. "Why, I reckoned we should sort of leave our cards as we pass by. Sort of bed down and see how much fun we can have with our rifles. That bunch is livin' too soft, looks like. Let's stir 'em up a little."

Gamble chuckled. "Let's go!"

Threading down the little-used horse trail, Gamble took them into a position among some gigantic boulders on a rise overlooking the ranch. Red swung down, his eyes glinting.

"Joe," he said grimly, "I'm goin' to like this job!" Dropping to the ground he leveled his Winchester between two boulders. A horse was tied to the hitch rail. Even at this distance they could see the dark stains of sweat. That horse had been ridden within the past few minutes.

Carefully aiming at the hitch rail, Red fired. The sharp spang of the rifle sounded, and almost with the sound the horse reared sharply. Frightened by the bullet that smashed the hitch rail, the animal jerked back, snapping the rail off, and then the horse dashed off, carrying its head high.

A man rushed from the door of the house and started for the horse, and Red instantly put a bullet in the ground beside him. With a frightened yelp, the man turned so swiftly that he lost balance and sprawled at full length on the ground. Red turned his rifle to the ranch house and proceeded to knock the glass out of a window. Joe Gamble joined the proceedings by firing two shots through the door, then shooting the windows out of the bunkhouse.

Aiming at the well rope, Red cut it near the wheel on the third shot, dropping the bucket into the well, from which it would have to be fished before the owner could get any more water. Gamble fired two bullets into the water trough in the corral, letting water out on the ground. He sent another searching bullet into the bunkhouse, and then together they hammered the door of the ranch house through which the running man had just gone. Another window was smashed out, and then they fired at the old chimney, ventilating it with holes.

A shot answered from a broken window, and both men let go at the spot as if on signal. The rifle barrel vanished instantly.

Grinning, Red drew back. "Let's go on to Agate, Joe," he said. "Those fellers ain't so happy about now, believe you me!"

In the ranch house of the 8 Boxed H, Jack Bolt got up from the floor, his face dark with bitter fury. Angrily he glared at the smashed windows. A bullet had found his water bucket and rained it on the floor. His coffeepot had been knocked almost from his hand. A picture on the wall was splintered, the door punctured by bullets, and Grat, who had been talking with him, had a scratch on his face from a flying splinter.

Peering from the door, they glimpsed in the door of the bunkhouse the figure of Bones, also taking stock of the situation. "Maybe they are gone," Grat suggested. "I thought I heard horses a minute ago."

"They shot the windows out!" Bones yelled. "Who was that?"

Jack Bolt stepped outside and glared towards the ridge from which the firing had come. "How should I know?" he demanded. "There was more than one."

"Fightin' that outfit ain't goin' to be no fun," Bones suggested suddenly. "Those hombres could shoot!"

"Cain't be Cassidy," Grat said. "He was in Agate the other night."

Abel Garson showed his head in the door, glancing fearfully towards the ridge. "It was that Red Connors and Joe Gamble," he said. "That was what I come out to tell you about."

"Then why didn't you?" Bolt whirled on the loafer, his eyes deadly. "Why didn't you come out with it?"

"Well"—Garson rubbed his palms on his chaps—"I hadn't

eaten nothin' and when I saw that grub I just sort of piled in. I was fixin' to tell you when the shootin' started."

"You sure that was Connors in town?" Grat demanded.

"Know him anywheres," Garson replied immediately, "and Joe Gamble was with him."

"I thought you told me that Connors was dead?" Bolt demanded, glaring at Grat.

"I did figure he was," Grat replied sullenly. "Last time anybody saw of him, he was ridin' for that ridge. We put a flock of lead in the trees after him, and when we caught his cayuse there was blood on his withers."

"Well, you're an idiot! I didn't send you out there for the exercise. And when I ask you for a report, I'm asking for what you *know*, not what you think!"

Jack Bolt stood still, studying the situation and finding nothing in it that pleased him. He had lived in security here, and now suddenly he had been fired upon. His toughs had been treated with contempt, his windows shot out, his whole ranch shot up, and the enemy had escaped without reprisal. Moreover, from their attitude, none of his boys seemed very eager to pursue. There had been no wild rush for horses, all of which was mute tribute to the shooting of the men who had fired on the ranch. He himself, he remembered, had been hugging the dusty floor only a few minutes ago while lead ricocheted about the room.

Now the two had gone off, probably on the road to Agate, hunting Hopalong Cassidy. If that outfit hadn't taken care of Hopalong, and the three joined forces, the rustlers would really be in trouble. But there was no chance of them trailing the cattle. He had often tried it himself, knowing the way they had gone, and he had consistently failed.

Thoughtfully he considered the situation. The big raid

would go ahead. A much bigger raid than the one currently under way. Moreover, if Hopalong, Red, and Joe had followed Aragon's men with the cattle, they must never be allowed to return.

"Bones," he said suddenly, "mount up and get into town. See Sim Aragon and tell him that Red and Gamble have started west after Hopalong. Tell him that none of them must come back. Get them—anyhow he wants to, but get them! I only ask that it be done west of the desert, so nobody will ever know. Understand?"

Bones nodded. "Yeah, I understand." Three men murdered, he thought, even as he answered Bolt. Good men, too. Bones had little imagination and less ethics, but he did possess a certain code of his own, and that code went against shooting a man in the back. It also demanded that a man fight his own battles. Bolt was showing no inclination to do any fighting at all. "All right," he agreed, "I'll ride in."

"I'll go along," Garson replied quickly. Ever since the shooting began he had been frightened, and the idea of riding back to Tascotal alone had frightened him even more. Besides, he would be more comfortable riding with Bones than with the others. The fat man was easygoing and not much inclined to run into trouble.

Bones started off towards the corral, and Bolt stared after Garson. He disliked the man even while he used him as a spy. There was nothing stable about Garson, nothing worth any kind of a gamble. It would never do to trust him, and Jack Bolt did not. As a matter of fact, he trusted no one but himself.

He watched the two ride off towards town in the twilight, and then he walked back to the house. A wind had started to blow and dust sifted in the broken window. Like a ghost house. Startled at the thought, he looked hastily around. He was not actually superstitious, he told himself, but such thoughts disturbed him. Gloomily he stared at the windows. He would have to get new ones in town, and that would mean questions. It would also excite comment from those he did business with, and in no time the story would be all over the country. Some suspicion that Red and Joe Gamble had just reason would be sure to remain.

Joe Gamble disturbed him.

Red Connors and Hopalong Cassidy were strangers in the country, and both had the reputation of being fighters. If such men were killed, there would be little surprise, nor would too many questions be asked; but Joe Gamble was a steady, serious cowhand with a good reputation—a hard-working man known to be honest and not a drinker.

Nevertheless, there was nothing else to be done. All three men must be killed, and the sooner the better. He walked the floor of his cabin restlessly, then gave it up. The very sight of the broken windows acted as a warning. He was now in danger himself. Courageous enough, he had allowed himself to let all that slip into the past, and for several years now he had been telling himself that he was the brains. Let others get shot at, not him.

"Boss?" It was Grat. "That outfit sure did us up brown. They clipped the rope on the well bucket and she's stuck down there."

"Well, get it out!" Bolt was impatient. "The fool who left the well hole so small should have been shot! Can't you hook the bail?"

"We're tryin'. Meanwhile there's no water. Even the trough is run dry."

Jack Bolt walked out into the ranch yard. It was growing late. He stared at the trail towards town, chewing at his under-lip. Maybe he should ride over to see the Gibsons. How much, if anything, did they know? Pod had run off, but that had been caused by Hopalong, and the gunfighter might not have said anything about Bolt's connection with the rustling—if he knew anything.

Sue Gibson— He scowled. She was a pretty girl, and they had danced together more than once. Maybe that was an easier way to get the cattle and the ranch—especially with her father laid up in bed. Anyway, he would ride over, be frank with them, and see what came of that. Frankness, he had learned, was disarming, and he might actually win Sue to his side. At least it was worth the chance while he was waiting for Sim Aragon to handle Cassidy for him.

He mounted up and rode off while Grat glared after him. The Breed and Slim were working over the well. "Get busy, you two!" Grat snarled. "The boss has ridden off and left this to us. A lot he cares if we never get a drink!"

Surprised, the others looked at him, and made more angry, he stalked off across the yard. He saddled his own horse, then stopped. Where would he go?

To the creek. It was not far off, and he could at least get a bucket of water there and fill all their canteens. He hesitated again. "How's it look, Slim?"

"Jammed up for fair. We'll have to bust the bucket, I reckon."

"Let it go till morning. Hitch up the team and load a couple of barrels. We'll go to the creek after water. That blasted Connors! That was him, and I know it! Nobody else could cut a rope at that distance."

Slim mopped the sweat from his face. "Don't reckon they could. He missed a couple himself. There's a bullet in the frame and the shiv wheel has been jimmied up. That Connors, he's a whiz with a rifle."

"Get the barrels loaded. I'm scoutin' around a little. You head for the creek."

Jack Bolt rode on, following the winding trail towards the wide range of the 3TL. The farther he rode, the more he wondered if this was not the best way after all. He did not hesitate to admit the truth to himself. The gunfire and the hum of lead had done something to him. Four years or so of absence from gunfighting and killing had changed his thinking. Cowering on the floor, hearing the bullets punch through the walls of his cabin, knowing that any one of them could mean death, had put something into him that had gone clear to the bottom of his mind and his stomach. He did not like being shot at. When he was younger he had been heedless. He had believed the bullet had not been made that would kill him. Death had seemed fantastically far away.

It was always that way when you were young. Well, he was older now and knew that death was no respecter of persons. There had to be an easier way. He had brains, and it was time to use them.

The moon was rising when he came within sight of the 3TL buildings.

CHAPTER 10

Fight in the Badlands

Circling the hot springs, Hopalong Cassidy walked the palouse back into the hills, keeping close watch on the country as he approached it. That an ambush might await him at any point, he was well aware. The horse he rode was one of the best he had ever ridden, but they had been on the move constantly now for some days, and he found himself wishing he was riding his favorite mount, the white gelding Topper.

The morning sun was bright and only beginning to grow warm. The tracks of the cattle were plainer now, and it was obvious that Pete and his men had caught up with the herd. Here and there a cow track partly obliterated one of the tracks Hopalong had memorized farther back along the trail.

Now the herd was in High Rock with its sheer walls towering four to five hundred feet above the trail. Rye grass grew along the floor of the canyon, which was narrow through much of its length but widening at intervals. Occasionally there were pools of water. Twice Hopalong allowed the palouse to crop the grass and drink while he scouted ahead on foot, alert for a trap. Here and there the old tracks of covered wagons were plainly visible, and in places had been gutted out and cut deeper by rains. Suddenly, in a wide-open space overgrown with tall grass, Hopalong found that the trail had petered out.

Puzzled, he circled around. Here and there he found the tracks of a single animal or, in a few cases, of two or three, but the herd seemed to have vanished into the tall grass, growing saddle-high to the horse he rode. Suddenly Hopalong heard the sound of a calf bawling nearby!

Searching around, Hopalong first found an 8 Box H steer, and if the brand was worked over, it was an excellent job. When he found it, the calf was standing with its mother near a tangle of brush that grew against the canyon wall. The brand on the full-grown cow was freshly burned, but the work had been so carefully done that it would be impossible to tell, without killing and skinning her, if it had been worked over. He pressed on, and although he found a few other scattered cattle, the trail of the main body of the herd had vanished.

Carefully he scouted the edges of the canyon but could find no trail out. Yellow Rock Canyon showed the trail of only one steer. Hopalong scowled and rode back to a spring in a cleft of the rocky wall. It was already growing dark, for he had spent most of the afternoon looking for the trail. Picking dry wood from a nest around the roots of a shrub, Hopalong built his fire and made supper. As he ate he considered the entire situation and what had happened.

Despite his search he could find no exact place where the trail began to peter out. It was as if the herd had gradually dwindled until the few remaining cattle had been scattered here in the upper reaches of the High Rock.

Daylight found him pushing on, and disregarding the dwindling herd and the missing cattle, he pushed on towards Coyote Springs. One horseman had come this far, the man riding the slue-gaited mustang. There was water in the springs, although nearby Massacre Lakes were only vast dry beds. He had seen no tracks of cattle this far north, but after a while he made camp on the sand near the springs. In the morning he would head back towards the south.

Red Connors stared through the dimming light. "You sure this is the way? Those tracks look like Hoppy's, all right, but he's sure doin' a lot of wanderin' around."

"Perhaps he's lost their trail," Gamble suggested. "We lost it miles back. A while back one of our boys struck the trail of a herd up here once and then lost it completely, just like it vanished into thin air."

The two rode on, and then Gamble drew up suddenly. "Fire ahead. Off there to the right."

Swinging their horses, both men rode towards the fire, but were still some thirty yards from it and could see nothing of its builder when a cool voice said, "Ride right up to the fire and get down facing it, so I can see your faces."

"Hoppy!" Red said. "Found yuh!"

"How are you, Red? You two get down. I'll put on the coffee. What are you doing up this far?"

"Followin' you. What did you think?" Red grinned. "We were afraid you'd get caught by these rustlers."

"Did you see Frank Gillespie? I sent him back to the 3TL. They were alone back there."

"No, we didn't see him, but then we didn't stop at the ranch either. We stopped only a few minutes in Agate. Talked with an old fossil named Sourdough. From what he said, you turned plumb salty in that town, Hoppy."

"I'm in more trouble now," Hopalong replied, then explained. "And the way things now look," he finished, "I've lost the trail. My idea was to head south down Long Valley and try to cut their trail on the west. They didn't come north, and they certainly wouldn't turn back towards the east—not unless they cross the border into Idaho."

Hopalong studied Connors thoughtfully. "Are you sure you are in shape for this kind of a ride? You lost a lot of blood."

"In shape?" Red Connors snorted. "I could outride you the best day you ever saw, and without half tryin'. As far as that lost blood is concerned, I could lose twice that much and still lock horns with this outfit you are chasin'."

Cassidy chuckled. "You hear that?" he asked Gamble. "This souwegian is so hardheaded he wouldn't move camp for a prairie fire. Like Lanky used to say, he's full-grown in the body, but kind of puny in the head."

"A lot you got to say," Red growled. "I could name some times you were sure glad to see me around!"

"You can bet your life on that," Hopalong agreed.

Daylight found all three men in the saddle. Hopalong led off, the palouse seeming none the worse for his days of hard riding. If ever a horse had a love for moving, it was this one. Several miles to the west, beyond Massacre Creek and looming above the dry lakes of the same name, was Painted Point, a landmark that stood out boldly against the sky, marking the opening into Long Valley.

"We'll head for that Point," Hopalong suggested, "and then we'll fan out and scout for sign to see if we can find any tracks this far north. If we can't, we'll ride south until we do. It's a cinch that herd had to come west or north, and if we keep moving we'll cut their sign."

"What beats me," Red exclaimed, "is how they got out of

High Rock. That herd just seemed to peter out. We saw the tracks and we followed them a ways. Of course we never scouted that country as thoroughly as you did, but we could see the tracks just fadin' out."

The sun was hot, and they headed west. "That hombre seems to be heading the same way," Hopalong said, indicating the tracks. "He was with the herd."

Yet scarcely a mile farther the mysterious rider turned north across the vast expanse of the dry lakes, pointing toward distant Yellow Peak. Hopalong hesitated, then shook his head. "Let him go. We'll ride south as we planned."

Yet he was growing worried. He did not like the idea of being away from the 3TL for so long a time with the country in the mess it was. Frank Gillespie was there, but he was not enough. But to return now meant a long ride back, and if they could locate the herd or even find the trail they had taken after leaving High Rock, they would be much better off.

Rounding the Point, they faced the wide expanse of Long Valley. At this point it looked to be all of nine or ten miles to the far side—not an easy distance for three men to cover and keep in touch with each other. The only possible way was to ride diagonally across the valley, and when upon the other side to cut back, checking all water holes and any tracks they encountered.

Hours later Red Connors joined Hopalong at a butte in the valley's center. "Gamble's comin' up," he said. "We didn't find a thing."

"No luck for me, either." Hopalong rubbed his jaw. "Our best bet's right ahead, at Pinto Springs. There's water there, enough for a herd. I've seen some cattle tracks headed that way, too. Mostly strays, I guess."

"It's bad," Gamble explained, worried. "The springs lie close to a butte, but they can't be seen from this direction until we are mighty close. I don't like it even a little."

"Yes, I see what you mean. If they have a man atop that butte or the long mesa this side of there, he could have been watching us for the last hour or so, if he had a glass."

Red squinted at the towering buttes before them. The air danced with heat waves, and he mopped his face, then pulled his hat low to enable him to see clearer. The two buttes rose high above the level of the plain. "A man with a rifle up there could sure make it mean for us," he agreed. "You got any water left, Hoppy?"

"I filled up at the last water hole. I've still got about two thirds of a canteen."

"Mine's nearly empty," Gamble said ruefully. "There wasn't anything but alkali over where I was. How about you, Red?"

"About half," he said grimly. "A man with a rifle could hold us off, keep us away from that water hole for a long time."

"He'll have to fight if he does!" Hopalong replied shortly. "Let's go!"

They rode on, accompanied by a little dust cloud of their own making. More and more Hopalong was sure that wherever the missing herd had been taken, it had not been to this valley. At least, not to remain here. Grass was scarce and water scarcer, and while in a wetter year this might be and probably was good grazing land, it was far from that now. A few cattle might eke out a precarious existence, but no large herd would do so. Yet if the herd had come through Long Valley's lower end, Pinto Springs would be the most likely spot to water.

They rounded a corner of the butte and suddenly Red yelled, "Look out!"

Swinging his horse to the left as he did so, Hopalong got a fleeting glimpse of sunlight on a rifle barrel and then something whipped by his head, and an instant later he heard the bark of the rifle. Racing for the rocks, Hopalong kept going straight ahead. He knew that he would soon be so close to the butte that any rifleman atop it would have to rise from concealment to get him in his sights, and unless he was badly mistaken, that would be the end of things for him.

The rifle bellowed again, the shot coming from high up on the butte, but now Hopalong was closer and racing for the water hole. Off to one side Joe Gamble had swung behind a low hill and Red had vanished in the rocks. There was another shot and Red's rifle spoke from behind him, and then Cassidy was in the shadow of the butte. A volley of shots rang out ahead of him, and his palouse stumbled and went headlong, throwing Hopalong to the ground!

Even as he hit, a shot struck near him, and Hoppy continued to roll until he lay flat against the side of a boulder. Bitterly he stared back at the palouse, fearing the horse was dead. But after a moment the horse started to get up, and he saw a red streak along the animal's neck. Evidently the bullet had stung the horse and it had made a misstep. Another bullet spanged against the rock where he lay, and another ricocheted near him. Helpless to return the fire, he lay still.

His rifle was in the scabbard on the palouse, who had struggled erect and walked off, stopping in the shade of some rocks where some bunch grass remained green. The horse was about thirty yards off, but an immeasurable distance when faced with the thought of an expert marksman less than two hundred yards away.

The sun was blazing down and Hopalong studied the terrain with a thoughtful eye. The boulder behind which he lay was only barely high enough to offer cover for him, and the position could easily be rendered impossible if one of the riflemen should work his way to the left, for then Hopalong would be within sight and it would be only one more shot and Hopalong would be out of the picture, and for good.

He winked the trickling sweat from his eyes and turned his head carefully to the left. The nearest cover in that direction was the boulder where the palouse was sheltered—a veritable nest of rocks and brush where a dozen men might easily conceal themselves—yet that thirty yards of interval was almost certain suicide. On the other side the rocks were small and scattered, but not twenty yards away there was a shallow depression.

Hesitating, Hopalong decided that he must take a chance. Unquestionably, the riflemen who were sniping at them would realize that he could be outflanked, and if he was to move, it must be now. Gun in hand, he squirmed along the sand and managed to move to the next rock. Here he had no more than an inch of clearance above his head. A bullet splintered the rock and tugged at his sombrero. Gathering himself, he lunged in a crouching run for three steps, then dived. He landed in a cloud of sand and dust, bullets raining around him.

Grimly he checked his position and found himself scarcely better off, but the shallow place was much closer now. From between two rocks he studied the situation where the riflemen were concealed. Suddenly a boot heel showed. Under no misapprehensions as to the range of his pistol, he knew it could easily carry that far, even though it was of uncertain accuracy at the range. Holding the Colt high, he fired. Sand splashed inches short, but the rustler jerked his foot back.

Behind him Red's rifle bellowed and a man cried out. Then the yell died away into a burst of sullen cursing. Red fired again and the curses ended in a yelp of surprise and fury. Hopalong crawled along the sand, made the shallow place, and rolled into it. Here he was safe from rifle fire, and he checked his Colts, thumbing shells into the one fired.

Carefully he took stock of his position. Red was still shooting, so he was all right. But there had been no sign of life from Joe Gamble, and he might have been injured. On the other hand, he might be just scouting for a good position.

The rustlers were apparently gathered in a cluster of rocks at the foot of the four-hundred-foot cliffs to the butte. There were ways up those cliffs, for here and there were steep or completely vertical chimneys that seemed to offer access to the top, but these would be in direct line of fire from Red. Somewhere behind those rocks, and probably around the turn of the butte, would be the outlaws' horses. Getting to his feet, Hopalong started moving swiftly down the shallow place in which he now found himself.

This depression was evidently an old wash that somehow had been closed off to water and gradually filled in by wind-blown sand mingled with drift and fallen rock. It ran past the butte pointing down the valley, but at one place it seemed to come within a few yards of the butte's shoulder. If he could get there without being noticed, Hopalong Cassidy would then find himself behind the attackers and probably in the vicinity of their horses.

Moving swiftly, and listening to the methodical boom of Red's rifle, Hopalong followed the filled-in draw, safe from either observation or fire. It took him all of fifteen minutes to reach his goal, and as he neared it he slowed his pace. Mopping sweat from his face, he listened attentively for any sound, but there was nothing. Peering through a clump of greasewood, he studied the lay of the land.

Here, as elsewhere, the foot of the cliff was piled with slabs of broken rock, yet there was no sign of the horses or of any tracks here. In a quick dash Hopalong made the shelter of the cliff and stopped to catch his breath. The boom of Red's rifle and the occasional rattle of the outlaws' guns sounded faintly here, partly cut off by the shoulder of the butte. Now Hopalong moved forward, holding close against the cliff and so avoiding the worst of the rocks. He had been climbing slightly and was now probably above the outlaws, but still there was no sign of their horses.

Suddenly, below him and some distance ahead, he saw a man dash from a cluster of rocks and dart towards him. Instantly Hopalong grabbed his gun and fired from the hip. The bullet caught the man in the knee evidently, for his leg buckled under him and he fell, plunging face downward in the sand, his rifle sliding ahead of him.

Wildly he grabbed for the gun but Hopalong put a bullet in the sand almost at his fingertips. The man jerked back his hand as if stung.

"You can get hurt," Cassidy commented dryly. "Better toss your pistols down there with your rifle, and don't try anything funny. You're out of this fight now, if you play it smart."

The man looked up at Hopalong, his swarthy face dark with fury. "You'll get killed," he promised. "They got too many for you."

Hopalong shrugged. "Toss your guns down here," he said, "and let me worry about getting killed. If we have to start a Boot Hill here, don't let yours be the first grave."

Sullenly the man unbuckled his belt and tossed his guns down beside his rifle. "My leg's busted," he said then. "You sure nailed me." His eyes rolled off to his right, and Hopalong was instantly all attention. He was aware that all firing had ceased. That this was due to his own shots he did not doubt. Both Red Connors and the outlaws would be in doubt as to what course to adopt.

The outlaws made up their minds first. . . .

CHAPTER 11

Hopalong's Ruse

Quick movement showed among the rocks, and a bullet spattered stone near Hoppy's face. He fired instantly, and the outlaw ducked with an oath. Hopalong fired again, then backed up, dropped to all fours, and scrambled for the gun belts and rifle. The wounded outlaw stared at him with reluctant admiration.

"You sure picked a dilly of a scrap," he said. "What happened to Vila?"

"He'll be all right. He laid for me and stopped some lead."

"He'll kill you," the outlaw promised matter-of-factly. "You got a match?"

Hopalong reached into his shirt pocket for his matches and tossed them to the wounded man. "I'll take those back," he said, "but light up."

The outlaw returned the matches. There was still no sound. The afternoon was hot and still. Sweat trickled down Hopalong's face. "You better fix up that bad leg," he said, "right now."

"Yeah." The dark-faced man straightened up a little. "Looks like I'm ridin' out of the money in this show."

A tentative shot clipped the greasewood over their heads, but Hopalong waited, taking his time. Soon a man would be sent to investigate. Hopalong wondered again about the horses of the rustlers and considered asking, then realized he could not expect a truthful answer, if any at all. Yet there was always a way, even if a devious one.

"You may be stuck here a long time," he suggested to the wounded man. "Those hombres aren't going to get out of here in a hurry."

"Uh-huh, I expect so," the outlaw agreed.

"Hope you had your canteen behind those rocks," Hoppy suggested. "You'll get mighty dry."

"Hey?" The wounded man's head came around sharply. "That's so!" He swore bitterly. "And my canteen is on my saddle!"

"Shucks!" Hopalong replied carelessly. "No need to fret. I'll get it for you. I've no mind to see a man die of thirst."

"Would you do that?" The outlaw was incredulous. "Say, that would be mighty fine! The horses are right back of that tall pine you can see yonder. You—" He broke off suddenly, seeing the sudden gleam in Hopalong's eyes. "Aw, that was what you wanted all the time! Sucked me in, didn't you?"

Cassidy grinned at him and winked. He was listening to a faint dragging sound in the sand. "Sure, but don't you worry. I'll get your canteen to you so long as you don't try to warn anybody. If you do that, I'll come back here and blow all your brains out through your ears!"

The dragging sound had stopped. It seemed to come from the rocks before him. Somewhere off to the north Red's rifle boomed. He had moved, obviously. Two shots replied, and then Red fired again. Knowing Connors's skill with the rifle,

Hopalong knew that somebody was feeling mighty uncomfortable. Red Connors never fired without effect.

Hopalong shucked his captured pistol after returning his own to his belt. Then he buckled the gun belt around his shoulder and under the opposite arm, making a bandolier of it. Then, with the Colt in his right hand and the Winchester in his left, he started to move toward where he had last heard that dragging sound.

He laid a course for the tall pine and crawled forward. Then he stopped and listened. There it was again, the sound of chaps or jeans dragging over sand. He left the Winchester on the ground and cautiously got to his feet. Then, with the Colt in his right hand, he gripped the ends of his fingers into a crevice in the rock and swung himself around in a crouching position, gun ready. A bullet blasted almost in his face, and then he fired. The outlaw slid to the ground. It was the big man Hopalong had seen in the saloon at Agate. Hoppy's bullet had cut deep into the scalp, laying the bone of the skull white and bare. But the man was still alive.

Stripping him of guns, Hopalong lifted them and threw them into the brush a dozen feet away. As they hit the brush two guns blasted, and then somebody grunted and there were signs of a furious struggle. Scrambling through the rocks, Hopalong brought up short.

Joe Gamble, blood trickling down his face, was slugging furiously with a husky rustler. Seeing Hopalong, the rustler jerked back and grabbed for iron, but Gamble threw a high right that flattened his nose and the man staggered. Instantly Joe was after him, swinging wild punches with both hands, and the rustler hit the ground on his knees.

Stripping him of guns, Hopalong wheeled and ran for the

tall pine. Yet even as he charged through the brush a shot whipped by his head and a bay horse lunged by him so close that he was spun off balance and fell back into the clutching fingers of a manzanita. Struggling erect, he heard Joe Gamble's gun roaring, and then silence.

"Got away!" Gamble said disgustedly. "We had 'em outflanked, too!"

"What about Red?" Hoppy demanded. "See him?"

The Winchester barked, then again, and they saw Red stand up and wave his hat. He had fired two shots after the departing outlaws. Their trap had backfired; two of their men were wounded and the other had taken a beating. At least three had pulled out in that final rush.

"Got away," Gamble repeated irritably.

"Let them go," Cassidy replied carelessly. "We got out of their trap and gave them a taste of trouble. Let them go and think it over. This will give them something to worry about, and we can pick up their trail again."

Connors rode up, leading Gamble's horse. Hopalong started back through the rocks after the palouse. He turned, remembering the wounded men.

"Better pick 'em up," he said, "especially the one with the broken leg. He'll have to have care or he might lose it."

The palouse nickered softly as he approached, and Hopalong smiled. "Glad to see me, boy? No more than I am to see you. That Dan Keating knew how to pick a horse."

Red was waiting for him when he returned. "We found the gent with the busted leg, but the other two took out. One of them left plenty of blood behind."

"That one got his skull grazed, Red," Hopalong replied. "He lost blood, and probably had a serious concussion. Well, now they've gone, it's their own problem about how they get help. We're going on after the herd."

"Know where they are?" Red squinted his eyes at the sun. "Unless you do we'd better camp at Pinto Springs. We'll never get far at this hour."

Cassidy nodded. "All right, only let Gamble make the coffee. Yours always tastes like alkali mixed with sulphur."

"Mine does?" Connors growled. "What about that brown stuff you make? You never could make coffee near as good as me, Hoppy, and you know it. I could teach you plenty."

"You couldn't teach a setting hen to cluck!" Hopalong laughed, winking at Gamble. "As long as you're herding cattle you're all right, but let you get even a half-mile away from a cow herd and you couldn't drive nails into a snowbank."

He turned to Gamble again. "Come on, compadre, we'll let Red stoke up the fire while we rustle some grub. That bacon and sourdough bread is all right, but I saw some sage hens out here on the edge of the rocks. They size up better to me."

Dusk fell and the shadow of the buttes grew tall. Joe Gamble concealed the horses in a clump of brush near the springs and made his own bed close to them. Hopalong found a space in a cluster of rocks and then returned to the fire. It was blazing cheerfully, and Gamble had taken over the cooking.

"We're due west of Soldier Meadows," he commented. "That outfit must have found a way to bring the herd through Little High Rock without leavin' any tracks."

"No chance," Hopalong said. "I looked that ground over carefully. There's got to be another way. Right now what I want to know is not how they got this far, but where they went."

"What's west of here?" Red demanded. "Could they have gone that way?"

"California line's over there a ways," Gamble mused. "They might have a hangout in Surprise Valley. It's just over the mountains yonder."

"We'll take a look tomorrow." Hopalong filled his cup with coffee. "We'll start first thing in the morning."

Sim Aragon was not sitting by a fire on this night. He had heard from Jack Bolt, and Bolt's impatience irritated him. Bolt was, he decided, getting skittish. There was nothing to worry about. With Cassidy, Connors, and Gamble all trailing herd, catching up to them would be simple indeed, and once caught up, the situation could be handled with guns.

Aragon had no particular confidence in his brother Pete as a fighter. Pete was the cattleman of the crowd, and although he could handle a gun well enough, he was not in the same class as Sim or Jack Bolt. It was Pete's responsibility to get the cattle over the state line and conceal them in Wall Canyon, where they could not be found. Always before he had managed to leave no trail. They had been careful to leave none, as they wanted no suspicion directed their way, and so far they had been successful.

Sim Aragon had three men with him, all hardened outlaws. Pete would have more. Cassidy and his friends were following the herd, and he would close up on them and from there on the job would be short, not too sweet, but very effective. This country was so remote there was small chance of anybody ever finding any of the three, even if they were left to be found, and Sim Aragon had decided that they would not be. They would be killed, then dumped into one of the sinkholes or hot springs. After that the boiling water would take care of them and no identification would be possible. So far as the world would know, the three could be said to have left the country.

He could see no flaw in the plan. Pete would close them off on the west while he came up behind with his men. They would be trapped and disposed of. It was that easy. Manuel was at his elbow—Manuel, who loved to kill. Not so very fast with a gun, but very deadly with any weapon, as vicious and tough as a Gila monster.

They moved out of Tascotal and took the road to Agate. Sourdough saw them there, and his old face was grim when they dismounted. Nobody needed to tell him that Hopalong Cassidy's number was up. He had gone off into the west after Pete Aragon, and here was Sim closing in on him. At Agate, Sim was joined by Vila, his hands much better and the hatred within him increased.

Sourdough looked across at his old enemy Mormon John when the outlaws went into the saloon. After serving them, Mormon John came to the door and Sourdough crossed the street. They stood together, not talking. Both men knew what would happen now, for these were not the first men to be followed by the Aragons into that wilderness to the west.

It was almost midnight, and the outlaws were still loafing at the saloon, when Sourdough heard the pound of approaching hoofs. A horse swung onto the street and the rider pulled up. Peering from his dark window, the old man saw the rider almost fall from his horse. The man was named Walters, and he rode with the Aragons. His shirt was red with blood and there seemed to be a patch on the side of his head. The man pushed through the door into the saloon.

Sim Aragon turned, and his eyes glinted. "What's happened?" he demanded. "What hit you?"

"Cassidy!" Walters gasped. "Gimme a drink!" He tossed off a shot of whiskey, then swallowed. "We thought we had him trapped, but that outfit are scrappers. They busted out, wounded me, beat up Perk, and busted Cardoza's leg."

"What about Pete?"

"Him and the others, they rode back to the herd. Cassidy was at Pinto Springs when I left."

Sim Aragon's face was ugly. "We leave at daylight," he said. "And then we'll settle that hombre's hash."

CHAPTER 12

Cattle Tracks

Once in the saddle, Hopalong Cassidy turned to watch Red mount up. Joe Gamble kicked sand over the remnants of their fire and then swung into the leather. The sky was gray only along the horizon, and here in the shadow of the butte it was still dark. Somewhere far off a sage hen called softly, and the palouse pawed impatiently at the ground, eager to be going.

Moving off, Hopalong led the way, scouting at once for tracks. The fleeing outlaws had headed southward yesterday— or had it been a little to the west?

"There's a big boxed valley southwest of us," Gamble suggested. "It has two creeks in it, Fox and Cottonwood. I don't know how much water they carry, if any at all. I was in there once when there was water, all right, but that could have been temporary."

"We'll try it," Hopalong decided. "They might not run right for the herd, anyway. By now they know we can read sign, so they may try to lead us astray. Where's the opening?"

"You can't see it from here," Gamble explained. "We ride southeast towards that big point of rock, then west."

To left and right the mountains lifted high and the valley grew narrower as they rode forward. Then it widened out, and they swung westward. A careful search of the boxed valley brought no results. No tracks could be found except those of an occasional lone steer or a group of two or three. While following one of these trails just on chance, Hopalong said suddenly, "You know, I've figured this out, I think."

"What's that?" Red demanded. "Must be mighty simple if you figured it out."

Hopalong shrugged. "It's simple enough. All the way along I've been trying to decide how they managed to get that herd out of High Rock Canyon. I still don't know just where it was done, but I do know how it was done. When they hit some of that sand back there where the tracks weren't well defined, they kept one part of the herd moving, then took the rest off into a branch canyon on the real trail to where they were going.

"Then as they moved along they let first one steer and then another fall behind or trail off by himself until the herd had dwindled to nothing. By bunching a few cattle and getting them to mill a little, they could make some of that trail look like a big herd had come over it. Later, when they had time, they could pick up those strays. Some of them would probably head back towards the main herd, anyway."

"But where could they get out of High Rock?" Gamble was puzzled. "I didn't see any tracks to speak of in Little High Rock."

"That's right," Hopalong agreed, "but that Yellow Rock Canyon could have been investigated more thoroughly. If there was a trail out of there to the west, that would be the likely spot. Anyway, I'd bet a good coon hide they came this way."

"Could be," Red agreed. "Maybe you aren't so dumb as I

thought, Hoppy. It could be under that hair of yours you've really got some brains."

Hopalong drew up, his eyes scanning the mountainside before them. "There's a trail to high ground," he said. "Let's take it. If we get up high enough we may be able to see over a lot of country."

A switchback trail led up the steep cedar-covered mountainside. There were no tracks here and this was evidently a long-unused trail, but obviously it had led to somewhere. Pausing to let their horses rest, Hopalong looked back down the trail at the thin green thread of Cottonwood and Fox creeks. Even from this height, which often gave visibility to trails unseen on the valley floors, nothing was visible that could have been made by a cattle herd.

"Wonder how Gibson's gettin' along?" Gamble wondered. "Think they'll make any trouble for him?"

"I doubt it," Hopalong said, although he was more worried than he wanted to confess. "Sue is with him, and you know what bothering a woman means in this country. It's not often you'll get even a bad man to lay a hand on a woman or endanger one."

"Gillespie with him?" Gamble asked.

"He should be. He left me to go back."

"I'd feel better," Red muttered, "if I knew where Sim Aragon was. They nearly got me once, and I want my chance at them."

"You'll get it," Hopalong said. "They won't quit now. They have too much at stake."

They started on, letting the horses take their own pace. The hill grew steeper, and once they had to dismount and roll a boulder off the mountainside. It went crashing down, hit a rock ledge, and bounded far out into space before rolling on. They were now almost eight thousand feet up, and a half mile higher than the valley that lay below them. The air was clear and fresh, and the sun not yet hot.

They reached the top and paused again, their eyes sweeping a broad plateau. Ahead was a peak that towered some distance above them. Far and away to the westward the distant mountain ranges lost themselves in a purple mist, giving the impression of a vast basin that lay between. Hopalong Cassidy sat his horse and looked with care at that country. Those distant ranges were in California. A man having a herd over there would be reasonably safe from the law. State lines were beginning to make a lot of difference—especially if that man had a good reputation on his own side of the line. Thinking that over, Hopalong remembered their conversation of the previous day and the suggestion that the thief might be building an honest-looking herd somewhere over there.

"You ever been over in there, Gamble?"

"No. Heard some about it, though. There's a grand big valley on the California side. Surprise Valley, they call it. Some forty-niner named it when they came through the mountains and saw it there. Mighty purty, I hear. Sometimes there's lakes in it, although mostly they are dry. Anyway, there's lots of good grass and some water. Farther west there's more."

"Where was Fandango Pass?"

"Not far from here. Named it for a party of forty-niners who had a dance to celebrate their crossing of the mountains. While they were doin' the fandango the Injuns came down on 'em and wiped them out."

Hopalong led the way across the plateau. They were riding north now, but the way west seemed blocked off. There was rugged terrain that fell away for three or four miles and then appeared to end in a steep declivity. There might be a way down, but their present trail was leading them north, and that should enable them to cut the rustlers' path soon.

At noon they camped at the foot of a smooth, black-faced rock and ate quickly. There was water here, and they refilled their canteens from the flowing spring while the horses drank from a pool.

"If we don't find them quick," Gamble said, "we'll have to find some grub. We're about out of it."

"Maybe I can get a deer," Red suggested. "I spotted a couple back along the line."

"We won't leave the cattle now," Hopalong replied seriously. "If we do, a dust storm or rain may wipe out their tracks. We're closing in on them, I think." He looked at the sun. "High noon. That gives us several hours to find their trail. I think we're heading just right. The cattle had to go somewhere, and we should cut it, riding like we are."

Red was cleaning his Winchester. He stuck a thumbnail in the breech and peered down the barrel, then drew a final cleaning patch through it. "Whenever you're ready," he said, "I am."

Before them the plateau was a long, almost level sweep of thin soil over rock ledges, while here and there jumbles of granite boulders lay scattered as though dropped from an overloaded basket. On the northern rim there were upthrusts of flame-shaped rock, girdled at the base with the green of vegetation growing where the shade had held moisture.

No cattle tracks were here, only the droppings of deer and the sign of rabbits or an occasional badger. They flushed a sage hen and killed it, drawing it before moving on. The plateau seemed to fall away in a series of long steps, each of them a half-mile wide, gradually sloping away before the final crop. Vegetation grew thicker—mountain mahogany and occasional manzanita and pine. Upon the slopes of low hills were thick groves of close-ranked aspen, their trunks a gray screen that permitted no penetration.

The sun's rays beat down upon them, and Cassidy saw Red's shirt growing dark with sweat. He grinned at the older man. "Hot!" he said.

Red snorted. "You call this hot? And you been in Sonora? Why, one time I saw a coyote chasin' a jackrabbit down in Texas and it was so hot they were both walkin'!" Red mopped his brow. "Although this here climate is sort of warmish now and again."

Several minutes passed when there was no sound but the clop-clopping of their horses' hoofs, and then Red continued, "Speakin' of that coyote and the rabbit he was chasin', I do recall they were both packin' canteens. There's dry lakes down thataway where even the fish hibernate durin' dry weather. They bury themselves in the mud and sleep until it rains enough to get swimmin' water."

Joe Gamble lit a cigarette and looked patiently at Hopalong, who grinned. "Sometime you want to get Red to tell you about the rifle he had that would shoot around hills."

"I'd like to hear it," Gamble agreed, sober-faced. "I have heard tell of rifles like that, but I never did come up to one. They might be good to have against some of those grizzlies we have in these mountains over in California. They grow bears over there that will outweigh a longhorn bull. Gibson killed one a few years back and they made a hide mattress for the whole roundup crew. They would just spread out the hide and the whole outfit bedded down on it. Finally had to give it up, though."

Red Connors turned, narrow-eyed with suspicion, but knowing that it was his role to ask. "Why?" he demanded.

"Well, we got to havin' our roundups in rougher country, and the trail wound around so much we couldn't get the two wagons over 'em. It took," he continued, looking off across the plateau, "two wagons hitched tandem and six head of oxen to haul that hide!"

Red snorted his disgust at such a story, but before he could speak, Gamble added, "That was the bear that durned near shot me."

"Shot you?" Red played along. "How's that?"

"Well, I was out at the line cabin on Forty Mile and it was about daylight when I heard something snufflin' outside the cabin door. Ever' time that bear snuffled, the suction drawed the carpet two inches under the door!"

"Anyway, I seen I was in for trouble, so I got down my old Spencer and jacked a shell into the chamber. I didn't have any idea of goin' out where he was, but if that bear turned the cabin over to see what was under it, I aimed to get one good shot, anyway. Those bears turn cabins over lookin' for food just like any other bear would turn over a dead log lookin' for grubs.

"Mebbe this here bear wasn't hungry. Anyway, he soon started off, and I opened the door mighty careful. For a while I had a hard time figurin' which was him and which was the barn, the light bein' dim like it was. Then I spotted him. I could tell the difference because he was movin'.

"Now, big as they are, those bears are the quickest-movin' things that live, an' I knowed I had to make that first shot count. But that bear was headin' straight away from me, so I just throwed down on his tail and squeezed off my shot.

"You see, Red, that bear turned so quick that the bullet come out the front end of him an' hit the doorjamb right over my head! Yessir! Right over my head! I always have wondered whether he really meant it that way or if he was just stung by the bullet. Took me a couple of hours to get the splinters out of my hair."

Red glared. "I was tellin' the truth," he growled. "Not no windy story."

Joe Gamble's eyes widened with innocence. "Why, you don't doubt me, do you?"

Red's eyes suddenly gleamed. "You said at first that Gibson killed that bear! Now you say you shot him!"

"Sure"—Gamble was undisturbed—"he did kill him. That shot that I fired just put a hole through him." He yawned. "Fact is, that bear kept us in meat and honey all one winter."

"Honey?" Red was bewildered. He came from a country of tall stories, but the possibilities of this one seemed endless. "What d'you mean—honey?"

"Sure. You see, that was a Spencer fifty-six I shot into that bear. Well, yuh know how big a hole one of them fifty-six caliber cartridges makes in a bear or anything it hits? This hole was so big that a bunch of swarmin' bees hived up in it, and when Gibson finally killed that bear the hole was stuffed full of honey!"

Hopalong chuckled and Red spat. "I wished you could meet Lanky," Red said grimly. "I'd like to hear you tell him that story."

"Tell you all about that bear sometime," Gamble said. "It's a long story."

Hopalong drew up suddenly. From where he sat he could see past the brink of the cliff that divided them from the valley of Duck Flat. Far below them they could see scattered black dots on the endless gray-green carpet of the valley. "There's some cattle," he said with satisfaction, "and it's my bet they're ours!"

Their eyes searched the rim for some way down, but there

was no possible way that they could see. "Might as well keep ridin'," Red suggested. "And hope this path comes down off here somehow or other."

Hopalong nodded, and they started on. Scarcely a mile farther the trail dipped down into a hollow and then descended swiftly. "This is it!" Gamble suddenly exclaimed exultantly. "Look!"

The trail they were following led to the bottom of a canyon several hundred feet lower, and from the east another trail joined it, and on that trail, even at this distance, they could see evidence of recent travel. The grass was plastered down in a manner such as could only mean a considerable herd of cattle.

It was almost an hour before they reached the bottom of the canyon. Now there was no possible doubt—the trail here was well marked and plain for all to see. A large herd had gone through here, coming over the saddle from the east.

"Sure as shootin'!" Red exclaimed with satisfaction. "Pinto Springs is northeast of here! That bunch took the herd right through Yellow Rock, like you figured, and brought 'em across here."

"They weren't the first, either," Hopalong added. "There's plenty of sign. I'd say a good many herds have been brought in this way."

"Then we better pin our ears back and ride quiet," Connors said, lowering his voice as he spoke. "Those outlaws can be anywhere along here now."

Hopalong shucked his guns and checked both, rolling the cylinders and fitting an extra cartridge into the two normally empty chambers. Red had his Winchester across his saddle before him, as did Joe Gamble. All rode with wary attention.

In the canyon's bottom there was shadow along the walls. No wind stirred here, no slightest cooling breath of air. It was hot, close, and utterly still. Hopalong's mouth felt dry and he looked carefully from right to left, his eyes never still, studying every fold in the rock, every boulder, every possible hiding place.

"How far do you reckon it is to the valley?" Gamble asked suddenly.

"Five miles," Red said, "or about that."

"Just about," Hopalong agreed.

"Ridin' out of here tonight?" Red studied Hopalong thoughtfully. Much as he argued with his friend, he knew his judgment was excellent in such cases. He had never yet seen a situation Hopalong got into that he couldn't get out of. Although never for the world would he have admitted it, he relied very much on the younger man's judgment and knew it was safe to do so.

"No," Hopalong said finally. "Not unless we slip out under cover of darkness. We hole up right here in the canyon."

"I've heard of this canyon," Gamble said. "There's two branch canyons right opposite to each other. They should be close by. We can take the one on the north. It branches back at the end, and in either of those branches we'll be safe from observation."

"Suppose we're bein' followed?" Red asked suddenly. "I got an uneasy feelin'."

Cassidy shot a keen glance at his friend.

"Could be," Hopalong agreed. "By this time they should have heard that I had a run-in with the rustlers at Agate. Vila would have told them."

"You know that means trouble," Red said glumly. "They'll figure this is just the place to get rid of you. Nobody ever rides out here. There hasn't been anybody in this country in years. Nobody but those rustlers and a few wanderin' Modocs."

"There! A little ahead," Joe said, "the canyon branches."

They studied the ground. Although night was still an hour away, the shadows were growing in these gorges along the mountainside. Yet here, opening to the setting sun, the earth under them could easily be seen. No tracks turned into either of the branch canyons. After a mile the side canyon branched again, and they took the turn to the left and followed it back. The walls drew close and high. The canyon was cool here, and where a shelf of rock provided the shelter of an overhang, Hopalong drew up and swung down.

Suddenly he realized how tired he was. For days, it seemed, he had been riding endless hours, and now that riding was catching up to him. Red stumbled a little as he reached the ground. Then all three men stripped saddles and bridles from their horses and picketed them on the grass that grew plentifully here in the shadows. Hopalong gathered an armful of dry wood and carried it to where Gamble was digging out the grub. Joe looked blankly at it. "Not much coffee, and enough flour for a thin bit of bread. One sage hen."

Red shrugged. "We've had less, a few times. We'll make out."

CHAPTER 13

Slanders

Pensively, Sue Gibson stood on the porch, watching the sun's last rays over the mountains in the west. A door slammed at the bunkhouse, and she looked up to see Frank Gillespie coming toward her. The one loyal hand who remained on the ranch shook his head ruefully.

"No news may be good news," he said, "but it's still no news. I wish we could hear something."

"Yes," she said, "if we could hear anything! Anything at all!"

Frank hesitated, then shoved his hat back on his head. "I saw you had a caller the other night."

"Yes, it was Jack Bolt. He was very friendly."

"He always is." Gillespie's opinion of Bolt's friendship was obvious.

"I believe we've made a mistake about him, Frank. He was very nice. He offered to help any way he could."

Gillespie stopped chewing, then spat. "Ma'am, don't you be taken in by him. You can't trust him."

"What is there against him?" Sue protested. "He offered to protect our herds. Said he could send some of the boys over to watch them. He said that if he failed I could have enough of his own cows to make up my losses."

"He said that?" Gillespie was incredulous. "I wouldn't trust him."

Sue Gibson was silent, but irritated, too. After all, what was there against Bolt? Only the flimsiest suspicion, that was all. Her eyes drifted to the trail. He was coming over again tonight. Maybe he would have some news of Hopalong. Inside, she heard her father calling.

"How is he?" Gillespie asked quickly.

"Better. He's sure he could be out and around now, and that it is absurd for him to be in bed. He's never been ill, you know, and he can't get used to the idea."

A horse sounded on the trail. Gillespie looked around quickly. His hand dropped to his gun, but Sue shook her head. "It's nothing to worry about. It's Jack Bolt."

Frank Gillespie stiffened and his face went hard. "I reckon," he said bitterly, as he turned away, "that's plenty to worry about!"

Bolt trotted his horse to the hitch rail and then slid down. "How are you, Sue? It's good to see you again."

"Thanks, Jack. Shall we go in?"

"Wait!" he protested. "Why can't we go for a walk? It's hot, and we could talk better."

"My father's calling, Jack. I couldn't leave him."

Concealing his irritation, Jack Bolt removed his hat and followed Sue into the house. After all, he told himself, there was no hurry. Sim Aragon would take care of Cassidy, and then he, Bolt, would have a free hand here and a lot of time. Gibson could stay out of the way or he would put him out of the way. This sudden change of plans suited him. There was no reason why he should not marry, and who could he find more attractive than Sue Gibson? And also she had a big ranch. Or would have when her father died.

The shooting that had taken place when Connors and Gamble raided the 8 Boxed H had done something to him. He was too smart to relish getting shot at. After all, why take chances when everything could be had without them? He had been a top gunman, and still was when it came to that, but what did anyone get by being a gunman? All one became was a target for every cheap reputation hunter who drifted through the country. It was a position he did not relish.

He had his own spread in California, but why not get the 3TL, too? It could be had, and easily. Sue Gibson would welcome his attentions, he was sure. A smooth-talking man, he found her alert and suspicious, but an evening of quiet, friendly talk had removed most of it, or so it seemed. Gibson had not liked his being there, he could see that, but the old man had said little, and he had been polite enough.

Gibson looked up as he entered, and Bolt saw a coldness come into his eyes. Nevertheless, Bolt smiled and spoke genially. "How are you tonight, Mr. Gibson? I thought I'd ride over and pay you two a visit. I am afraid I haven't always been a good neighbor, but when a man is down I like to help all I can."

"Thanks." Gibson spoke shortly, his eyes going to Sue. He was puzzled. What did his daughter see in this man?

"Heard anything of Hopalong?" Sue asked. "We've been worried."

"No"—Bolt measured his words with care—"I've heard nothing. You mustn't be worried, though. After all, both he and Red are drifters, and they are fighting men. It gets into the blood of such men and they never stop drifting and fighting. That Bar 20 outfit have always been troublemakers."

Gibson bristled. "Trouble for rustlers and thieves!" he retorted. "They've always been on the side of the law!"

Bolt shrugged. "You know them better than I do," he admitted. "Nevertheless, nobody can know if they have always been on the side of the law. And there has been plenty of killing, regardless. Some people say it has been needless killing."

"That ain't so!" Gibson exploded. "I won't have you comin' here runnin' down my friends!"

"I'm sorry. Perhaps I spoke too hastily." Nevertheless, Bolt saw a faint line of worry between Sue's eyes and realized that he had obtained the result he wanted. If he could undermine their trust in Hopalong he would be going far toward getting rid of the two—or, at least, in creating a doubt as to their intentions and actions. Such a doubt was enough to build on, he knew. Jack Bolt did not hope to convert Gibson, although he might make the older man waver in his loyalty. It was Sue of whom he was thinking.

Far from a handsome man, he was somehow attractive, and he was clever enough to give himself an air of quietness and to listen with respect when Sue talked. There was more flattery in his attitude than in any of his speeches. Jack Bolt had learned that it sometimes pays to be subtle.

Sue made coffee and they talked. He led her to speak of things close to her, and listened with attention and interested comment. When the opportunity offered, he did his own talking. "This country is growing, Sue, and it is becoming civilized. The old law of the gun and the noose must go. We need homes, schools, churches here, and we can have them, but before we can have peace we must be rid of those men who cling to the old way of doing things. Take Cassidy, for example; I have no doubt that he is, or has been, a fine man. I have no doubt that he has done a lot of good, but this is a time for due process of law, for order. Once a man establishes a pattern of action like Cassidy, he cannot change. Frankly, I admire the man, but he is a relic, a relic of a day that is gone. We must have peace on the range."

Despite herself, Sue listened and found her doubts growing. How could such a man as Bolt be in league with rustlers? Hating the thought of guns and killing, she was all too ready to be convinced. Several times she stole a look at the man's profile. There was something about him that repelled her, and yet, she told herself, that was unfair. Every man deserved a chance.

"I'll never believe any bad of Hoppy," she said. "I've known of him for too long a time. I've known too many good things he did."

"No doubt he has done good things, and no doubt he is, in his own way, a good man, but they say this Missouri outlaw Jesse James has done some good things, too. That didn't keep him from shooting down a schoolboy during a bank robbery. Shooting him down when he was carrying books and doing no more than trying to get out of the street.

"I know nothing against Cassidy," he continued smoothly, "but he is too free with his fists, too free with a gun. Right now he is off in the hills chasing men and hunting for trouble. He believes they are cattle thieves. But are they? Will they ever have a trial? Or will he shoot them down when they try to defend themselves?"

A cool wind stirred across the veranda, and Jack Bolt got to his feet. "You deserve the best, Sue. You could be anything you wish, and in this country there will be need of fine women as well as strong men. We need such people if we are to build the kind of world we want here."

Long after he was gone she heard his words in her ears,

and she walked restlessly in the ranch yard, or sat on the porch and worried. Hopalong remained in her mind, as he always had, but now her doubts had increased and she was no longer sure of herself.

Where was Hopalong? Gone somewhere with an idea of finding their missing cattle. That was what she knew and what she had heard. Would he find the cattle? And would there be killing?

She looked again towards the west. She had never gone far in that direction. Her father had often told her of the wild country beyond the mountains and along the California line and she had heard many stories of the earlier days here when the wagon trains had gone over the Applegate Cut-Off. How could Hopalong Cassidy hope to find any cattle driven into that wilderness of mountain and desert?

Her father was asleep when she returned to the house, and she looked at him for a long time. These were trying days for him. He was a man who had lived in the saddle, and he was now chained to a bed. Yet he was better, and soon he would be riding again. Knowing how many cattle seemed to be gone, she wondered how he would feel when he began to ride over the hills.

Faint and far off she heard a shot, then another, and several in a bunch. Running to the door, she stared off towards the northwest from where the shots had come. A hinge creaked and she saw Gillespie standing in the door of the bunkhouse, his face pointed towards the distant shots. He turned suddenly and went back inside. In a minute he was out, rifle in hand.

"What is it, Frank?" she asked quickly. "Where are you going?"

"Going?" His face was savage. "We're losin' more cows, that's what it is! They are runnin' 'em off now!"

"But what can you do, Frank? One man alone?"

"I can kill at least one of the dirty thieves!" he said bitterly.

"Don't go, Frank. Don't leave us alone. I'm afraid."

He hesitated, looking longingly towards the northwest. But in the vague light of the stars and the reflected light from the door Sue's face was drawn and pale.

"All right," he said reluctantly, "but we're losing cows."

It was noon the following day before they knew the worst. The range had been swept clean. Not only on the 3TL but on the 3F and the 4H spreads as well. Some time during the night a carefully planned raid had hit the three ranches and started what must have been a thousand head of cattle moving—and by daylight they had completely disappeared.

CHAPTER 14

Change of Route

From the ridge above their camp Hopalong Cassidy scouted the wide plain of Duck Flat by means of his glasses. At a rough estimate, no less than six hundred head of cattle were grazing in the range of his vision, yet the sparse grass could not possibly feed such a herd for long. Obviously this was but a way station on the drive, and the cattle would be moved before long.

To the south the flat widened out into a broad valley, but in that direction Hopalong could see what appeared to be riders who moved ceaselessly to prevent any cattle from drifting south. To the north the flat narrowed to a channel that was scarcely a half-mile wide, and through that channel the cattle would be driven. From what Gamble and Sourdough had told him, north of there lay Surprise Valley, and the California state line. For a long time Hopalong Cassidy studied that channel and its rocky walls. He took the glasses from his eyes and considered the situation with care.

He was a thoughtful man and knew very well that a few minutes of thinking often saved no end of trouble. An intelligent man never took an unnecessary risk, and Hopalong had long since learned the foolishness of moving without careful consideration.

It was not enough merely to recover this herd. The real necessity was to discover where the previous cattle had been taken and who was behind the stealing. Yet there was no reason to allow all these cattle to get away. His problem now was to discover how to save part of the cattle while letting the remainder of the herd go through so it could be followed.

Somewhere nearby would be the ranch that was the destination of the cattle. Watching the distant, faint blue smoke that marked the rustlers' camp, Hopalong was suddenly startled to see a bunch of horsemen emerge from the mouth of the very canyon down which they had come on the previous night. These riders pushed on across the valley, and Hopalong turned his field glasses upon them.

The riders were closer than the camp, and while he could make out no features, he could see the men were heavily armed. This would probably be Sim Aragon.

Hopalong's eyes narrowed with speculation. Then Aragon had followed, and had undoubtedly seen their tracks. Had he discovered their turnoff into the branch canyon? It was improbable, as the floor of the canyon at that point was rock washed bare of sand. Hence he probably believed them somewhere in the valley. Only by the good fortune of taking the branch canyon had they avoided being set upon by Sim and his riders.

Now the rustlers outnumbered them by at least three to one, too great odds to meet in any open combat. If they fought at all, it must be from shelter and with a good getaway planned. Yet fighting in that way could only delay the end, not change it. The arrival of Sim Aragon and his riders altered the whole situation. The best thing, then, was to let the herd go through and follow it.

The sun was rising, although it was not over the mountains behind him as yet. The rocks on which he lay had lost most of their nightly chill, and the sky was growing clearer. Shielding the glass to forbid any possible reflection, Hopalong again studied the distant camp. Within a half hour the riders would reach the camp. Give them another half hour of conversation, mutual recriminations, and argument, and it would be at least an hour before they were in the saddle and moving.

Sliding off the rock where he had been watching, Hopalong descended the steep path he had found and in a few minutes was beside the fire.

Red Connors grinned as he approached. "Better grab your cup, Hoppy; this is the best coffee I've had in months!"

"And the last you'll have on this trip!" Gamble said grimly. "This is the end of our grub."

"We'll find some," Hopalong said. "In fact I was thinking about that very thing."

He explained then what he had seen from above, outlining the lay of the land and the probable line of departure to be taken by the cattle and the rustlers. He also told them of the arrival of the other riders and his conviction that these were Sim Aragon and his men.

"We could stop the herd at that channel," Hoppy said. "We might hold it there, though if they stampeded it through we'd have to give up. That's probably what they would try. They've enough men to keep that herd moving while some of them scouted around and shot it out with us. We'll not gain that way."

"How about the grub?" Red interrupted. "We can't go on without it."

Hopalong explained briefly, and as he talked the other two men began to grin. Hurriedly completing their light breakfast, they broke camp and mounted up. Hopalong led off, taking the route by which they had come, retracing their ride back up the canyon and to the plateau across which they had advanced to the canyon.

"There's a high red butte," Hopalong explained, "that stands out by itself. We can find their camp by that."

The red butte kept showing itself from time to time as they headed south. By the time they reached the cliff opposite it, Red had sighted his glasses on the camp beyond.

"The bunch is gone," he said gleefully. "Only one man there, breakin' camp. We'll have to hurry."

Gamble had scouted ahead. "Looks like a deer trail here," he called softly. "Let's go."

Riding down the steep trail, they looked up the valley. From the dust it was evident that the rustlers had already started the cattle moving. Hopalong turned south, and describing a narrow half circle, keeping to low ground and washes, he led the way across the flat towards the camp. As they came out of the wash they saw the cook about to put his foot in the stirrup. He was scarcely fifty yards away.

Walking their horses for silence, the three riders rode up on him, fanning out a little to prevent escape. "All right!" Hopalong spoke sharply. "Up with your hands! Reach for your gun and you're a dead man!"

Joe Gamble had shaken out a loop, and as the rustler spun his horse the loop shot out. With a surprised yelp the rustler grabbed for his gun, but the noose dropped and whipped tight. He left his saddle and hit the dust with a bounce. Instantly Red

Connors was on the ground and racing for him. The man struggled to his feet, but Gamble tightened up on the rope, and in the space of half a minute the rustler was hog-tied and helpless, but not silent. He cursed them bitterly.

"I'll kill you for this!" he shouted. "I'll kill you!"

Hopalong shook his head, his eyes cold. "You aren't killing anybody. Haul him back in the shade, Red. We'll leave him here. If we remember him we'll come back and pick him up when the show is over."

"Hey!" The cook's voice turned anxious. "You ain't leavin' me here? What if a catamount shows up?"

"No panther or mountain lion would bother you," Hopalong replied shortly. "They're particular about what they eat!" He turned to Red. "Take his canteen. There's water here, and in time he'll get loose. He can drink then, but he can't travel without a canteen."

Rounding up the two pack mules, the three headed off for the mountains. Behind them the sound of curses, yells, and finally pleading died away.

Returning to the hills, the riders split up the food into three packs, which they divided among themselves. Then they cached the remainder, including ammunition and a considerable length of wire.

Gamble nodded at it. "What's that for, I wonder?"

Hopalong chuckled. "You haven't been in Texas, Joe. That's baling wire, but they use it for changing brands. It's better than a running iron, and all you have to do is twist it into the shape you want. You can alter brands so perfectly there's no way to tell, short of killing and skinning the animal. That accounts for the smooth brands we've seen."

"What now?" Connors demanded. "Those hombres will be already movin' that herd through the gap."

"Let 'em move it," Hoppy said briefly. "We'll ride along and watch."

"I wish I knew how things were back at the ranch," Red said worriedly. "Jack Bolt ain't in this outfit, nor any of that bunch of his. Did you see Grat or Bones?"

"No sign of 'em," Gamble agreed.

Topping a low rise, they could see the dust of the herd up ahead, and it was moving steadily through the gap into Surprise Valley. Hopalong studied them briefly, then turned to the others.

"No use all three of us being here," he said. "I'm riding back to the 3TL. Red, you are good on a trail; you keep after this herd and see what happens to them. Joe, why don't you head back, pick up that hombre we tied, and then get him to lend you a hand with that Cardoza—the one we bedded down with the broken leg. He may be in bad shape by now, and he should be back where a doctor can work on him. I'll hit it out at top speed for the ranch."

"Good idea," Connors said. "I'll follow the cattle. Don't you worry none about that."

"How about you, Gamble?"

The cowhand hesitated, then grinned ruefully. "All right, but I'll probably miss out on the fightin'. What do you want me to do after I get those hombres back to Tascotal?"

"Better check with your boss, then hightail for the 3TL. If I am not there I'll leave word for you. Now I'm going to rattle my hocks out of here."

With a wave of his hand Cassidy was gone, putting the palouse into a canter that rapidly took him back down the trail. He rode steadily, stopping only to give the horse a brief rest, a taste of water and grass, then moving on. It was a good distance, and he wanted to keep moving.

By nightfall he was on the edge of Soldier Meadows, and, crossing, he made a quick camp in a notch among the rocks and close under the rise of the first bluff of the mountains. He was only a short distance from the hot springs, and he used one of them to provide water for coffee and cooking. Finally, when darkness was well fallen, he went to sleep.

He awakened with a start. By the look of the stars, the night was already far advanced and he had been sleeping for some time, but what had awakened him he could not imagine. The air was cool, almost cold, and the stars were very bright. He could smell the faint steamy odor of the hot springs and the freshness of grass. For a long time he lay with his eyes wide open, and then he caught the shadow of his horse's head etched sharply against the night. The palouse was standing with head erect, ears up, peering off into the night down the valley.

Hastily, Hopalong reached for his gun belts and buckled them on. Then he drew his Winchester close and hurriedly pulled on his boots. By the time he was on his feet and had his Winchester ready, only a few minutes had passed. On cat feet he crept down the little draw towards the open valley and paused there, looking out into the darkness, where he could discern nothing, could hear nothing. A cricket chirped with determination; somewhere a nighthawk called. And then he heard—cattle!

He stiffened. Cattle, here? Now? Scowling, he walked out a few steps from the rock and listened again. Then he heard the sound of the hoofs—a large herd, moving steadily up the valley towards him. It was unbelievable, but they were coming! Had the rustlers struck again? But the Aragons, or two of them at least, were already far over to the west. Suddenly his skin tightened.

If a herd was moving now, and nothing but a stolen herd would move at this hour, then Bolt's own men must be moving it! Here was all the evidence he would need—if Bolt himself was driving them!

Wheeling about, he ran for his camp and hastily saddled up, then threw together the few loose parts of his gear and tied them on behind his saddle. He was in the saddle and moving out across the meadows towards the herd when he saw the broad hat of the point man going by. The man did not see him, and despite the chance that he might be Bolt himself, Hopalong allowed him to continue. First he wanted a look at the cattle. This was a large herd, and if it had been stolen tonight, the brands would be unchanged.

Working his way into the outer edge of the herd, Hopalong bent low and struck a match, shielding it with his hands. Holding it against the animal's flanks, he saw the brand. Only an instant before the light flickered out.

3TL!

This, then, was a stolen herd, and there was no sense in allowing them to move it farther. Hopalong pushed out of the herd and then heard a yell up ahead:

"Slim! What you lightin' a match for? Durn you, don't you know you can see a match for miles on a night like this?"

"Aw, forget it!" Hopalong said. He made his voice sound ugly. "If you don't like it, go hang yourself!"

The point rider whipped around with a snarl. "You say that to me?" He pushed his horse forward. "You want trouble, you can have—" He gasped then. "Hey! You aren't Slim! You—" Hopalong struck swiftly with the barrel of his Colt, and the rustler grunted, then slid from the saddle.

Stooping and grabbing his collar, Hopalong dragged the unconscious man to the side and out of the way of the herd.

Then, deliberately, he took the point himself and began to work, turning the cattle ever so slightly from the trail they should have taken, turning the point of the herd due north and then northeast. Knowing the ways of cowhands, he knew that it might be some distance ahead before anyone rode up to ask any questions.

There was a good trail this way, and it would lead over a ridge and past the ruins of an old army camp and then back into the desert. By that time he hoped to have them headed due east and right back to the 3TL. Grinning despite the danger, he kept the herd moving, leading at times and talking to the cattle, but at times falling back to urge them on faster and faster.

CHAPTER 15

Treacherous Attack

The rustled cows were over six miles on their way before there was a sudden clatter of hoofs and Hopalong heard two racing horses coming up on the flank of the herd. There was no time for talking. If two men were coming, it meant that something was wrong, and it was always possible the man he had knocked out had come to and caught up with them. Turning hard right, he pointed the herd down the mountain and then raced down the opposite flank, wheeling at times to urge the herd on with shouts and blows of his hat. The cattle were nervous at the unexpected night move and they began to trot, then to run. With a thunder of hoofs they raced down the far side of the mountain toward the desert. There were frantic shots as men tried to turn them, but they had little effect.

Swinging into the drag of the herd, Hopalong saw one lone rustler bringing up the rear. Instantly, Hopalong let out a long Texas yell and fired two quick shots. The running herd broke into a wild stampede, and the startled rustler wheeled with a curse of rage and raced toward Hopalong. Holding his gun low, Hopalong waited. The rider jerked up his pistol and Hopalong fired. The rustler cursed and Hopalong charged at him. The man swung away and raced off. In the brief moment of passing, Hopalong saw that the man's hand was bloody.

The herd was running now, and he fired again and again; then, swinging his horse around, he reloaded his gun. Hopalong drew off, riding into the hills and cutting across the direction the herd had taken.

The two riders who had raced toward the point of the herd had been Grat and the Breed.

Neither had noticed the herd's change of direction for some time, and then it was the half-breed who grew uneasy. Finally he called Grat's attention to it, and after a few minutes of observation Grat saw that Pahute Peak was almost straight south of them. Furious at what he believed was Slim's negligence, he raced his horse toward the front of the herd and the Breed had followed. Then came the shots that stampeded the herd, and both men were swept along by the onrush of cattle. Neither was able to stop or escape from it, and they were carried on until the herd reached the desert on the far side, when the thick sand began to slow them down.

Black with fury, Grat started riding this way and that, trying to gather in his men. It was then that Pod came up, blood trickling from his lacerated scalp, and explained what had happened.

"Who was it?" Grat demanded hoarsely.

"I didn't get a look at him," Slim said, "only I noticed some spots on the horse, black against white."

"Hopalong Cassidy!" Pod Griffin exploded. "That was him! I had me a chance and I muffed it!" Furiously he slammed his hat to the sand. "And to think I could have killed him!"

"Or been killed," Grat replied dryly. He liked none of this. It was scarcely an hour to daylight now, and they could never get the herd out of the desert in time. They could never round them up, let alone get them over the pass and into California. Within an hour riders from the 3F and the other spreads would be coming. Reluctantly he turned to the others.

"We'd better clear out," he said bitterly. "If we don't we'll be caught red-handed."

"And leave these cattle?" Pod was incredulous. "You're crazy, man!"

"Crazy?" Grat glared at him. "I'd be crazy if I stuck here tryin' to round up this herd until a search party came up on me. You think I want to stretch hemp? You can have it, if you want! Me, I'm takin' out!"

"What'll Bolt say?"

"What he says won't save my neck if those boys get a rope on it!" Grat said emphatically. "Let's go!" Wheeling their horses, they started away at a rapid trot.

From the crest of the ridge behind them Hopalong saw the dark line of riders moving out. The distance was great, but he slid his Winchester from the scabbard for a parting shot, then gave it up. He had done enough. He had broken up the biggest mass cattle steal he had ever seen attempted. The cattle would drift back toward their own water, for there was none on the desert where they had been abandoned. And they had not far to go.

. . .

Pod Griffin's head ached abominably, and he was furious. Suddenly he slowed. "Grat, Hopalong Cassidy is back there somewhere. I'm goin' huntin' him."

"Don't be a fool!" Grat said angrily. "That curly wolf would have your hide on the fence before you knew what hit you!"

"Like blazes!" Pod's face was white with repressed fury. Grat could see the ugly look of hatred on him and suddenly made up his mind.

"Go ahead," he said, "but be careful. Take your time."

After all, why not? Hopalong needed killing. In fact, he had to be killed or they were through. Obviously, Pod Griffin was crazy with the desire for it—and there was just a chance he might succeed. Let him have his try. Feeling as he did, he was apt to do something reckless, and the farther away he was, the better for the rest of them.

Griffin turned and rode back toward the hills, and Hopalong, who had swung his own horse only a minute before, did not see him start back.

A few scattered cattle remained in the arm of the Black Rock that lay at the foot of Pahute. Hopalong was tired, and for the first time he realized how tired. Yet he started the cattle, and picking up more as he pressed on, headed them southward.

The sun lifted and grew warm. His muscles sagging with weariness and his hat pulled low, he dozed in the saddle, his body soaking up the heat. The palouse was tired and he walked wearily, little puffs of dust arising from each step. The strays, now augmented to some thirty head, moved placidly before him. Hopalong straightened up and blinked his eyes. Slowly his gaze circled the hills, then the empty desert, but there was nothing in sight. The weariness crept over him again, aided by the early warmth of the morning sun. He dozed.

Far back, not yet to the edge of Soldier Meadows, Pod Griffin rode. He rode like an Indian, well forward in the saddle, every sense alert. His mouth felt dry and there was a queer jumpy sensation in his stomach. Hopalong Cassidy might be anywhere, anywhere at all!

What was the matter? Was he afraid? Was he getting like some silly kid? After all, what was there to Hopalong Cassidy that was different from any other man? He had killed men. He had faced men with guns before. Why let this worry him?

Suppose Grat was scared. All of them were, for that matter. But Hopalong could be just an overrated reputation. Pod knew how those things grew. People already said he himself had killed more than twice the number he had actually slain. Not that Pod ever denied it, for he had no intention of denying it now or any other time. He liked the reputation of being a gunfighter, and if he killed Cassidy—his eyes suddenly brightened with determination—why, he would be the biggest man around!

And why take a chance? Why not just let him have it whenever he saw him? He could go up afterward and put Cassidy's gun in his hand. He could even fire a shot from it. He could make people believe he had killed the great Cassidy in a stand-up gun fight!

He was alone and so was Cassidy. Who would ever know the difference? For an instant he hesitated over the thought. Hopalong had friends. Red Connors, Mesquite Jenkins, some of the greatest fighting names of the West. Suppose they took it up?

Well, he reflected, suppose they did. He could watch, he could be careful. Then he could add their scalps to Hopalong's. Soon they would be talking of Wild Bill Hickok, John Wesley Hardin, and Pod Griffin!

His chest swelled and he saw himself striding down the street, pointed out in saloons, talked about, envied, and the interested object of attention for all the girls.

The sun was warm, and his horse stumbled and jerked him out of his dream. He had better ride with care or he would never get a chance. Thinking Hopalong Cassidy dead and actually killing him were two vastly different things. And the man might be anywhere. There was something to what Grat had said. A man did not get the reputation Hopalong had by doing nothing. And what had he told him? He had warned him out of the country!

If they met now—

Pod Griffin drew up and touched his lips with his tongue. Still, he had to go on now. What would they say if he came back with some wild story? Would they believe him? They would not. Only Cassidy dead would convince them.

The tracks of the cattle covered the sand. Here and there he could find the tracks of horses. Where was it Hopalong had struck him? His head ached and he could scarcely focus his eyes. His horse slowed and pulled toward the spring, and Pod let him walk there. After they drank they moved on, and emerged at last into the middle of Soldier Meadows with a clean sweep of the valley before them. Pod Griffin stiffened.

A herd of cattle, far off now, and moving ahead of a lone rider!

Cassidy!

Quickly he studied the situation. Hopalong Cassidy was alone. He was driving cattle. Soon he would be turning east after passing Pahute Peak, and a man with a rifle atop that ridge could have him in easy range. Furthermore, Hopalong would be unable to get up the ridge after him if he should miss. But he did not plan on missing. Slapping the spurs to his cayuse, he raced along the trail, taking a short cut over the ridge and back of Pahute Peak that would put him ahead of Cassidy in much less the distance the gun fighter would have to follow.

Hopalong Cassidy blinked his eyes open and stared ahead. All was quiet. The cattle walked placidly, content in the knowledge they were headed toward home. He looked around and saw nothing. Pahute Peak was behind him now, and a steep ridge lifted on his left. He watched the cattle walk, but his weariness, the warmth, and the rhythm of the walking horse had their way and he was dozing again.

High upon the ridge Pod Griffin wiped the sweat from his hands and took a new grip on the rifle. Hopalong Cassidy was less than four hundred yards away and coming nearer. Griffin swallowed and waited, his heart pounding, his mouth dry. As the palouse walked closer, following the gather of cattle, Pod Griffin lifted the rifle and cradled the heavy butt against his shoulder. He took a deep breath, put the sights on Hopalong's temple, held his breath, then fired!

Hopalong Cassidy slumped suddenly, then slid from the saddle and fell into the sand. Startled, the palouse backed away, and Hoppy's boot toe hung in a stirrup, then slipped free. The horse backed away, looked around uneasily, and then lowered his head to nose at the fallen man. The sickish-sweet smell of blood made the horse snort and back off. The bunched cattle had not stopped. They plodded on. The horse looked after them wishfully, then stood still. His bridle reins had fallen, and he knew his duty.

Overhead the sun blazed upon the black shirt of the fallen man. A buzzard wheeled in the brassy sky. Pod Griffin got to his feet. He was trembling like a leaf. "Got him!" he gasped. "I've killed Hopalong Cassidy!"

CHAPTER 16

Pod Griffin's Blunder

Jack Bolt's visit to the 3TL had not been made entirely because of his awakening interest in Sue Gibson and the possibilities presented by marriage to her. His presence either in the house or just leaving in the opposite direction would remove him from any possibility of suspicion.

This was the big raid and the last one, utilizing his own men and a few rough characters who would take their pay and drift on out of the country. His connections kept him in touch with such men, and they were often useful.

It was with high good humor that Bolt heard of the raid. Frank Gillespie could do nothing alone, and Bolt correctly surmised that Sue would not allow him to leave the headquarters. The 3F was too far from that part of the range to get men on the ground at once, and his men had their orders and could reach an adequate place of concealment before pursuit could be successfully organized.

Bolt arose the following morning in fine fettle. As he prepared breakfast he made further plans. He would ride over to the 3TL and complain about losing cattle; he would learn of their raid, then offer to use his men to ride after the cattle. He would fail to recover the herd, and he would be very regretful. This would place him in a good light with Sue. Later, after the marriage, he could restock the depleted range.

The first drive had by now reached Surprise Valley, and unless something very surprising had happened, Hopalong Cassidy and his friends were now dead or cornered and fighting for their lives. The second drive was well on its way, and by now their trail had vanished in the loose sand of the desert or the hard rock of the passes. No matter what happened, he was in the clear.

Sunlight bathed the trail as he started for the 3TL. When he came to the main road he was surprised to see a rider a short distance ahead, leading a magnificent white horse. The rider was a stubby man, grizzled and homely.

Riding alongside, Jack Bolt slowed his pace, unable to take his eyes from the led horse. "That's quite a horse," he said. "Who owns it?"

"This horse? Why, this here's Topper, Hopalong Cassidy's horse."

"I'll buy him," Bolt said. "I'll make you a good price."

"You crazy? There ain't enough money in the world to buy this horse from Cassidy."

"Well"—Bolt was reluctant to give up—"if anything happens to Hopalong, you bring that horse to me."

The stubby man chuckled. "Don't hold your breath. Hopalong doesn't let things happen to him. Why, if all the lead that had been shot at him was loaded on a ship, she'd sink right to the bottom."

Jack Bolt smiled uneasily. The man's confidence irritated him. What if the Aragons did fail to get Cassidy? What if he did come back? No matter how well a trail was covered it was never so well done that a clever man could not unravel the skein and find out where all the threads began and ended. Jack Bolt knew—he had left Texas just a few jumps ahead of a Ranger who was some shakes at unraveling crooked trails.

Shaking off his doubts, he rode on ahead and soon came in sight of the 3TL. There was no sign of life, and then just as he was growing puzzled he saw Sue come out of the house dressed for riding. Gillespie led her horse from the barn. Bolt scowled. Was she going to town or was she going to scout around herself? That was something he did not want, and yet— why not?

Riding together, he might advance his case much faster than in any other way. His eyes narrowed and he began to smile. That was just the ticket! To ride together!

Sue looked up as he rode into the yard. Her face was pale with worry. "We were raided last night, Mr. Bolt. I don't know how many head they got. Frank said it looked like they had stripped the range."

"Stripped it?" Bolt allowed just the right note of incredulity to creep into his voice. "Oh, no! It can't be that bad, Miss Sue! I'm sure it can't! I was just about to tell you that I lost cattle last night, too. But not over fifty head at most."

Gillespie stared hard at Bolt. "We lost plenty!" he said. "And when I can get free of this ranch I'm goin' huntin'!"

"Don't blame you," Bolt agreed affably. "I'm feeling the same way."

He turned to Sue. "You're riding—were you going to look over the ground?"

"Yes. I don't want Frank to go. He'd keep on going and maybe get killed for his pains. After all, he's the only friend we have here now."

Bolt looked offended. "Now, Miss Sue, I don't take that kindly. I've always thought myself a friend of yours, and there's nothing I wouldn't do for you."

She was contrite. "I'm sorry. I wasn't thinking."

Gillespie turned away with disgust written in every line of him. He watched them ride off with narrowed eyes. Maybe, he reflected, he was a fool, but if Jack Bolt was an honest man, he was next in line to be Emperor of China!

Some miles to the west Joe Gamble was moping along behind two captured outlaws—the still angry cook and Cardoza with his broken leg. The leg was now in splints, and Cardoza, despite the anguish it caused him, rode with infinite patience. Once, some years back, he had been an honest cowhand. Right now he was wishing he had known when he was well off.

Gamble brought up the rear, his rifle across the saddle in front of him. He rode warily, although taking plenty of time because of Cardoza's leg and the jolting caused by a faster pace. Gamble knew very well what his chances would be if he was caught with his prisoners. The Aragons were not noted for their mercy. All were killers.

The night before, he had heard distant shots, and that worried him, as they came from the direction Cassidy had taken. After a while he cut Cassidy's trail, but his own route for Tascotal was to the south, and he did not want to ride around with his prisoners. Almost three hours later he topped a rise and halted. Before him, drifting slowly towards the west, was a huge herd of cattle!

"What in blazes!" He stared, puzzled. No riders accompanied the cattle, and they were pushing across the desert, apparently following some course of their own.

"What do you make of that, Cardoza?" he asked wonderingly.

Cardoza spat. "Looks like somebody messed things up proper—or else they run into plenty of trouble."

"What do you mean?"

Cardoza made no reply, and the cook stared sullenly at the big herd. Gamble spoke to his horse and they started on. Rapidly they overtook the slow-moving herd, and the first brand Gamble saw was his own ranch, the 3F. Within a few minutes he had spotted cattle from the 4H and the 3TL. Apparently rustlers had tried a big drive and something had interrupted them. Remembering the shooting of the previous night, Gamble tightened his lips. Hopalong Cassidy must have encountered this herd. There had been a fight, but where was Hoppy now?

Cardoza was doing some thinking on his own. This was the boasted big drive, come to nothing. Something or somebody had stopped it and started the cattle back home; but if so, where were Grat and the others? Where was Cassidy? Had they killed each other in the shootout?

Gamble fell in behind the herd and urged them to a faster pace. Cardoza's broken leg was tied in place and he could ride fairly well. He swung out to one side and helped, as did the cook. Both were cattlemen first, and these things were almost second nature for them.

Suddenly, as they neared the edge of the desert, a group of riders topped the crest of the pass before them. Almost at once Gamble recognized the black horse his boss always rode, and beside him was Sue Gibson. His eyes narrowed. Jack Bolt was there too. Bolt's eyes flashed as they recognized Joe Gamble's two prisoners.

"Joe!" Dru Monaghan reined in his black. "What happened? Where did you get this herd?"

Sitting his horse, Joe Gamble told the story, only leaving out the present whereabouts of Red Connors. Seeing Jack Bolt there made up his mind on that. When Sue asked about the men, Joe shrugged.

"Don't know, ma'am. I reckon they tangled with the rustlers who were drivin' this herd. They either got killed or kept chasin' 'em, because this herd was sure enough alone and headed for home when I found 'em."

Another horseman had come quietly down the hill behind them, and now he spoke. Frank Gillespie had taken the arrival of the rider with Hopalong's horse as an excuse to ride out himself, leaving that tired cowhand to take care of Gibson.

"You said you lost cows, Bolt. I don't see any 8 Boxed H stock here."

Voices stilled suddenly. A horse stamped, but even the herd seemed willing to be silent. Jack Bolt turned cold inside, then looked over the heads of the men between them. "What do you mean by that?" he demanded.

"Nothin'." Gillespie was relaxed and easy, but his right hand lay on his thigh inches from his gun. "Only if you lost cows, it's mighty funny they ain't here. These are all 3F, 3TL, and 4H stock."

"Some of mine are there, probably. Anyway," Bolt objected, "we've no proof this is the whole herd. I sure lost cows last night."

Dru Monaghan looked at Gamble and saw his eyes on Bolt. For the first time suspicion came to the 3F owner. He looked Bolt over carefully. "Seems funny if you didn't," he said quietly. "This drive would have passed the corner of your place."

"What are you implying?" Bolt demanded.

"Nothin'." Dru Monaghan was short. "Nothin' at all. Only I'm curious."

"So am I." Gillespie persisted. He could see Jack Bolt's face hardening and the tension building up, but he was reckless of consequences. "I'm mighty curious. I reckon a few of us had better backtrack this herd and see just where these cows were driven and who was driving them."

Sue Gibson looked from one to the other, seeing the suspicion in their faces. She was suddenly angry.

"Why, what are you thinking of?" she demanded. "If you think that Jack had anything to do with this, you are as wrong as you can be. He was visiting at my home shortly before the raid, and he left in the opposite direction. You all know that country. He couldn't have circled around!"

Joe Gamble spoke for the first time. "Nobody said he had anything to do with it, ma'am. We were just wonderin' why he was so durned lucky. Anyway," he added, "we've got two rustlers, and maybe they can be persuaded to talk."

"I seen that Cardoza!" The speaker was a blunt-featured 3F hand. "He rides with Sim Aragon."

Cardoza said nothing. The cook shifted in the saddle and looked around at the gathering of cattlemen. His face was pale.

"Take me to the law," he said. "I want to talk to a sheriff!"

"He wants to talk to a sheriff," Gamble said. "Shall we let him talk before he hangs? Don't make much difference, does it?"

"Not a bit." Gillespie was staring at Bolt. "We'll get every man Jack of 'em, anyway."

"What happened to Cassidy?" Sue asked suddenly. "Where is he?"

"He started back before I did," Gamble admitted. "I figure it was him stampeded this herd away from the outlaws."

They sat silent, knowing what that could mean in the darkness. "Reckon some of us better have a look," Monaghan agreed. "Who wants to come?"

"I'll go, if Gamble will return to the ranch with Miss Sue," Gillespie said. "Should be somebody there. Anyway," he added, "Bolt will want to ride with you."

Jack Bolt's face flushed with anger. "Gillespie, you keep out of my affairs. You've talked about enough today. If you want trouble, start something!"

Gillespie smiled, but his face was cold. "Why, I reckon I'd like nothin' better, Bolt!"

Monaghan shoved his horse between them. "Cut it out!" he snapped harshly. "Gillespie, you come along if you like. Let Bolt go back to his spread. No sense havin' you two killin' each other."

He turned to Gamble. "Joe, you ride on home with Miss Sue. Stay there."

CHAPTER 17

Red Connors Reports

As finally decided, the group numbered five men. Others took the cattle and started them back. Jack Bolt was suddenly left alone. Turning his horse, his face dark with fury, he started back for his own ranch. Yet within him a tiny pulse of warning was pounding. This was getting close. Why did they suspect him? And that confounded Gillespie! His eyes narrowed. When his chance came he would kill him, but not now. Not now.

What could have happened? Their big drive was ruined, the herd turned loose and his men scattered.

When he came in sight of his own ranch he saw the horses in the corral. Then the men were back! By the red-hot hinges, he would see what had happened! He would know the reason why!

They sat on the porch. Grat was tipped back in a hide-covered chair, his tough, stubble-bearded face still dusty and grim. Slim, the Breed, Bones, and Pod Griffin.

It was this last one who took his eyes, for Pod was standing wide-legged in the middle of the porch. "Sure, he was fast," he sneered. "He was fast, but I beat him to it and downed him. If you don't believe it, go look at him!"

Grat looked up as Bolt swung down from his horse. Bolt glared at them. "You sure played hob!" he said viciously. "What happened? How could you lose that herd?"

"Now, boss," Grat began placatingly, "it was this—"

"It was Cassidy," Pod interrupted. The realization that he had killed the great Hopalong Cassidy was big within him. In his own eyes his stature had suddenly grown enormously. Why should he take a back seat for Grat? Or for any of them? Lording it around, the way they had been! "It was Hopalong. He busted into us and stampeded the herd. It could have happened to anybody. Grat wasn't at fault; nobody was. But don't you worry, it won't happen again! Not from Hopalong Cassidy!"

Pod Griffin ached to be asked why; he was standing there, his chest swelled, his eyes glowing. Jack Bolt did not notice. He was thinking only of the lost herd.

"Sheer incompetence!" he snapped. "And as for you, Griffin, when I want talk from you I'll ask for it."

Griffin was astonished. "You talk that way to me?" He was furious. "To *me*?" He took a step back. Already he was thinking of himself compared to Hardin and Billy the Kid. "You been comin' it big around here too durned long, Bolt! Hereafter you speak to me like a gentleman, or—"

Jack Bolt's fury suddenly focused. "Or what?" he demanded. He faced Pod Griffin, his hands ready. "Or what, you tinhorn?"

Pod Griffin was not an intelligent man. All the way back to the ranch he had been going over and over the idea that he had killed Hopalong Cassidy. In his mind's eye he saw himself acclaimed a great gunman. At first he merely realized that he could tell his own story of the killing and nobody would know the difference. Then he began to convince himself that Hopalong had seen him, had missed his chance. Back in his mind he knew the truth, but thinking over the times he had slung a gun and killed, he remembered that he had always been the fastest. How did he know he was not faster than Cassidy? Or Hardin, for that matter? Had he ever been beaten?

Bolt faced him along the length of the porch, and suddenly Pod Griffin knew that this was it—he had to show them. He could see their disbelief when he had told them. Now he would prove it!

"Why, you talk to me careful," he said, "or I'll kill you! I'll gun you—"

Bolt's hands flashed, and in that ghastly split-instant Pod Griffin knew the truth. It had come to him here, in this shadowed veranda smelling of old leather and tobacco smoke. In that flickering instant he saw Bolt's gun hand flash, saw the barrel sweep up, the black muzzle stare at him, saw it blossom with flame—and then he backed up slowly, sat down, and he was dead.

Grat stared at Griffin, then at Bolt. He was shocked and amazed. He had never dreamed the boss could draw as fast as that. And Griffin? He looked again. The gun had never cleared the holster.

Jack Bolt stepped back, his glittering eyes going from one to the other. "What got into him?" he demanded. "What's he been eatin'? Locoweed?"

Grat shook his head. "No, but he told us he'd killed Hopalong Cassidy."

"Killed him? Killed Cassidy?"

Bolt stared at the dead man. "Where? How did it happen? Did you see it?"

"Nobody saw it. He went back after him. Pod was sore

about the pistol whippin' Cassidy had given him, and he went back gunnin' for him. The next we knew, he pulled in here braggin' that Cassidy was dead."

"He was probably lyin'," Bolt said.

"Nope." Bones spoke up. "He sure must have done it, boss. You never saw anybody so blowed up over himself as he was. He didn't get that way by accident. Cassidy's dead, all right. I don't figure he beat him to the draw like he was tellin' us, but I figure he really got him."

Cassidy dead! Then where was Red Connors? Bolt's questions assured him that none of his men had seen Connors or any sign of him. Nor had Gamble mentioned him beyond the fact that Connors had taken part in the fight with Pete Aragon's men. Had Cassidy's friend been dead, he surely would have mentioned it, yet he had not. That meant that Connors was alive, and if not with Hopalong, where was he?

The answer to that was one that Jack Bolt did not at all like. Red Connors was logically the one to have followed the herd that was first stolen. In other words, there was every chance that he was now witnessing the transfer of the herd to his hands from the California ranch, and so was learning what not even his own men knew—that Bolt actually owned a ranch over the state line.

Impatiently, Bolt walked away from the conversation that had sprung up among the men. He heard them removing the body of Pod Griffin, and listened to the sounds of the picks in the hard ground as they prepared a grave for the dead man. A few hours before, all had been going well, and now his whole show was breaking up. If Cassidy was dead, then the sooner Red Connors was killed, the better. Could he rely upon Aragon for that?

Carefully he took stock of the situation. The big drive had

failed, and the ranchers were alerted. The other cattle were being followed by Connors, and the very fact that Gamble had not mentioned it indicated suspicion. Gillespie had openly implied his, and Monaghan was ready to listen, as were others. The situation here indicated that he had better pull in his horns and keep very quiet, then sell out when he had a good chance.

Four hours after the bullet had struck Hopalong Cassidy, the palouse began to grow impatient. He was a horse who liked to get somewhere, and standing around cropping the sparse grass did not appeal to him. The scattered cattle had gone on by themselves, heading toward home, and the palouse wanted to be moving on.

The fallen man lay unmoving, and the horse overcame his dislike to the blood smell and moved nearer. He pawed the earth, blew irritably, then nudged the fallen man with his nose.

Hopalong Cassidy's eyes opened to find gray earth within an inch of his face. At first he lay still, not realizing where he was or what had happened. He could feel the dust under his fingers, the dull throb in his skull, and the beginning coolness of evening. Then he heard the palouse.

"All right, boy," he said quietly. "Just a minute."

The horse's ears came up and he moved nearer, relieved that he was not alone.

Memory returned slowly, flowing like thick molasses into all the convolutions of Cassidy's brain. He had been driving a bunch of strays toward the 3TL. They were recovered cattle, recovered from rustlers. Then there had been a blow on the head. His fingers stirred and felt for his skull. There was blood on his forehead, and then he realized what had happened. The bullet had grazed the skin along his brow from side to side, striking a glancing blow as it struck, then skidding around. He squinted one eye then the other. Each could focus on the ground nearby and the horizon. . . . Maybe he was not badly hurt.

Was the ambusher watching now? Cassidy considered that, his wits sharpening. The chances were the man had gone on; hours must have passed since the shot was fired, as it was now quite late.

Carefully, testing his strength, Hopalong drew back and got his hands under him, pushing himself up, then to his knees. His head swam, and he looked around him. After an interval he caught the stirrup of his saddle and pulled himself erect. When he was on the horse he started south.

As he rode, his thoughts began to add up. Whoever had shot him believed him dead. He had fallen; he had not moved. Had they come near him they must not have examined him, or the job would have been finished. Hence he was believed to be dead.

There was a seep near the end of the rocks not a mile away, he recalled, and he headed for it. When there, he dismounted, stripped the saddle from the palouse, and picketed it. He built a very small fire, heated water, and bathed his head. Then he made coffee and fixed something to eat. It was almost ten by the time he could get into his blankets.

He awakened in the cold light of dawn and he was much refreshed. The ache in his head remained, and as he sat up it began to throb. He got up, fixed breakfast while keeping a sharp lookout, and just when he was breaking camp he saw a rider. Even at the distance he recognized Red Connors.

Connors rode up, stared at the broken skin across his brow, and chuckled. "That thick skull saved you again, did it?"

he said. "I reckon you couldn't drive a bullet into it no more than you could an idea."

"What did you find out?" Hopalong demanded. "Stop complaining and tell me that."

Red swung down and rescued the last of the coffee before Hopalong could throw it out. He drank from the pot. "Plenty! That Aragon outfit turned the cows over to some riders who were waitin' for 'em in Surprise Valley. Seven cowhands, their horses all wearin' Rafter D brands. The Aragon outfit turned around and headed back this way. I took to the hills and followed the cows. They went north and then west. They finally wound up in a little valley near Goose Lake. Fine range, good-lookin' outfit. None of these hombres looked familiar, so I took a chance and drifted down on 'em from the north."

Red drained the coffeepot and rinsed it out with hot water from a nearby spring. He dried the pot with a handful of grass, deliberately waiting.

"All right, you spavined, broken-down cow nurse," Hopalong growled good-naturedly. "Give me the information. That is, if you learned anything."

"Seems," Connors said, building a smoke, "that a gent name of Jack Bronson owns the Rafter D. He is stockin' up on cows, which he is buyin' in Wyomin' and drivin' across Nevada. The spread has added fifteen hundred head this year, almost that much last year—and the old stuff has been sold off. This Bronson figures on movin' in there to stay right soon. He has been driftin' around buyin' cattle in the last few years."

Red Connors drew deep on his cigarette.

"It sort of seemed to me that I remembered a man named Bronson from Colorado. They didn't think so, but they described him."

"Jack Bolt?"

"Uh-huh."

Both men were silent, then Cassidy asked, "How about these Rafter D hands? Were they rustlers?"

"Nope. I'd say they didn't know anything at all. One of them may suspect. He's a slim, gray-faced hombre with blue eyes. He just listened to them talk to me and said nothing. But once or twice I had the feelin' that he was smilin' and had figured a lot of things out."

Hopalong Cassidy swung into the saddle. "All right, Red. I guess we know all we need to know now. There's evidence to be had, and I guess we'd better head for Tascotal and the telegraph station."

"Why there?"

"Wire the sheriff over there near Goose Lake. We'll get him to hold those cattle for evidence. Let's go!"

"I reckon," Red said briefly, "it's all over but the shootin'!"

"Well, let's hope we can do it without much of that."

Red Connors snorted. "All right, you hope! I'll keep my gun ready! If you get through this without shootin', you'll be mighty lucky! Mighty lucky!"

CHAPTER 18

Crumbling Ambitions

Tascotal drowsed in the sun of a bright morning with one eye open for trouble. Even those less perceptive than the inhabitants of the cow town would have noted the air of tension that hung over the streets. Tascotal had no theater and no carnival. Aside from the weekly dances or occasional ranch parties, the town was without entertainment except in the occasional outbursts of violence.

Some of the boys had drifted in from even such outlying spots as Sod House Point and Bottle Hill. Cowhands from the neighboring ranches found excuses to head for town. Hopalong Cassidy was dead—that story had gone the rounds. Pod Griffin had killed him, and the stories of how it was done were many.

The story had also reached town somehow that Griffin himself was dead, slain in a gun battle with his boss, Jack Bolt.

Old hands who knew the background of Cassidy began to wonder if any of the Bar 20 outfit would show up, and they recalled that Red Connors was still unaccounted for. So the town waited, talked low, and kept their ears tuned for the slightest sound. Meanwhile, other rumors added fuel to the growing blaze.

There had been a gun battle west of town, and several men had been killed. Cardoza had a broken leg. A couple of the others of Sim Aragon's outfit had been wounded. A large herd of cattle had been found drifting, and much was being thought of the fact that no 8 Boxed H cattle were included.

Shortly before noon two riders appeared and rode swiftly down the street to the telegraph office at the railroad station, yet as they passed, men looked startled. Hopalong Cassidy and Red Connors! Abel Garson was leaning against an awning post before the express office. He stiffened, then mulled this new information over in his mind. If Cassidy was not dead, trouble was coming. He turned from the porch and ducked back for his saddle horse. This was news!

After sending his wire, Hopalong turned back to the street and stood there studying it for a long time. None of the outfit from the 8 Boxed H was in sight, and he could not see any of their horses. Nor were any of the Aragon crowd among the men along the street.

Sue Gibson came out of a store up the street, and Hopalong stepped down on the boardwalk and started toward her. It was an old walk, the boards gray and silvery, yet worn wherever a man might find a place to sit. Sue was walking slowly, watching the street, and at first she did not see Hopalong. When she did she stopped abruptly, then gave a glad cry and ran toward him.

"Hoppy!" she cried. "We were afraid you'd been killed!"

"Not me." He smiled at her excitement. "That must have been somebody else. How's your dad?"

"He's up. He's been walking with a cane. Just a few steps,

of course, but nevertheless he is up, and he's fretting to see you. Where have you been?"

"Chasing rustlers. Is Bolt in town?"

"You mean Jack?" Her face suddenly sobered. "Don't tell me you are like the others, Hoppy? That you think him a rustler?"

"I'm afraid I do," Hopalong replied carefully. "I'm afraid there isn't much doubt of it!"

"Oh, I don't believe that!" Her eyes flashed. "You're all too ready to accuse people. He seems so nice!"

Hopalong chuckled. "Ma'am, no man is all bad, nor is he bad all the time. There's nothing about being dishonest that has anything to do with politeness. Some of the worst men unhanged are polite, and they can carry on a conversation that no lady would ever take offense at. But that doesn't make them honest."

"Well," she retorted, "I don't believe he's guilty. Frank does, I know, and after we found the herd without any 8 Boxed H cattle, more of them were suspicious."

"You found the herd, then? Good. We started it back but didn't manage to stay with it. Red was off on another job, and—well, I got shot."

"Shot?" Sue was horrified. "How? Were you hurt? I mean—"

Carefully he removed his hat, and she stared at the crude bandage that covered the wound across his forehead at the roots of his hair. "It was a close thing," he said.

Red Connors had moved up beside him. "Hoppy," he said guardedly, "here comes Bolt now!"

"Don't say anything," Cassidy replied quickly. "Not until after we've heard from over there. I want to be sure all that evidence is safe."

She looked from one to the other. "Men are so dense!" she flared suddenly. "Why should you think Jack Bolt a rustler?"

Bolt was nearing them, and suddenly he realized who the man with Sue and Red Connors must be. He stopped only an instant. Then, his face a shade whiter, he walked towards them, smiling. Hopalong could see the sudden wariness in the rancher's eyes.

"Well, this is a surprise," Bolt said. "You must be Cassidy. We heard you'd been killed. Glad to see you're back and feeling all right."

Hopalong smiled. "Thanks, Mr. Bolt. I appreciate that. Mind telling me where you heard it?"

Bolt hesitated, seeing the trap. With careful fingers he drew out a small black cigar. "I can't"—his brow puckered thoughtfully—"recall. Everybody has been talking about it. I doubt," he added, "whether anybody actually knew anything. They probably surmised from your long absence that something had happened."

"Heard you had a fight yourself," Connors suggested.

"I?" Bolt waited, feeling his stomach tighten. "When was this?"

"With Pod Griffin. Heard you killed him."

Bolt hesitated. So one of his own men had talked? His eyes darkened, but he shrugged. "Oh, that? Yes, we had a fight. Something gave him an idea he was fast. I think"—he was growing more confident—"I think he must have been the one who shot at you, Cassidy. I think he thought he had killed you, and the idea gave him an exalted opinion of his ability. He forced a fight on me, and I killed him."

This was news to Sue Gibson. She looked again at Bolt. He had killed a man only a few hours before and had to be reminded of the fact. Could Cassidy be right? Was he a rustler? Her father disliked him; Frank disliked him. She shivered slightly, listening to their voices.

"If you remember who told you I was shot," Hopalong replied casually, "let me know. Only two people could know that. Myself and the man who shot me. I haven't told anybody until this conversation began with Sue. Wherever your story started, it started with the man who shot me."

"Then it must have been Griffin," Bolt replied shortly. "You don't suspect me, do you?"

"I don't suspect anything," Hopalong said, but the tone of his voice and that slight underlining of the word *suspect* worried Bolt. What did they know? What could they know?

Abel Garson was not far away, trying to signal him. Bolt nodded, then said, "Well, I've got to get around a little. See you. Adios, Sue."

Garson had turned away and walked towards his horse, which was tied at the corral. Bolt paused, lighted his cigarette, which had gone out, and then started casually towards his own horse. Garson was tightening his cinch.

"Cassidy's up to somethin'," Garson said. "When they rode in they went right to the station. Don't know what they did, but I figure they sent a wire."

Jack Bolt absorbed that, his mind working coolly. He stood there in the dust with the smell of the horse's sweaty flanks in his nostrils. What could they have discovered, and where had the wires gone? He considered going to the station, then dismissed that as unlikely of success; yet see those messages he must. His whole future might well hang upon them.

He was leaving his horse when he saw a man loafing in the shadows in back of the livery stable. The man motioned, and Bolt walked over to him. Manuel Aragon's eyes glittered.

"We lose thees cows, *si?*" Aragon shrugged. "Well, another time, maybe."

"Where's Sim?"

"They come soon. Seem ver' angree." Manuel spat. "Thees Cassidy—I would not want to be heem."

Bolt considered the situation and considered Manuel. He was the half-brother of Pete and Sim and had spent most of his life in Mexico. He was an able, deadly fighter, although he lacked Sim's gun skill. But no plan came to him. His head felt thick and for the first time he was genuinely worried. Before there had always seemed so many chances of victory, so few of failure. Now Hopalong Cassidy was in town, some of Sim's men had been taken prisoner, and their big drive had fizzled out to nothing.

His mind would not clear. The things that usually came so easily to his conniving brain now failed him. He had no plan, no idea of what to do. The feeling of disaster in the atmosphere increased and Jack Bolt felt as if the weather itself was expressing his feelings of doom. The air was sultry, heavy with heat, its usual dryness gone. The sky was vast and brassy, with no distinguishable features.

If he could get access to the telegraph station and check the messages . . .

He turned away, tossing a "See you later!" over his shoulder at Manuel. It would be a good idea to leave town, yet he hated to be away, for fear something would develop that he needed to know. Instead of going to the hills and awaiting darkness and a chance to force a way into the telegraph office, he would stay right here in town.

Crossing the street, he entered the saloon. Dru Monaghan was at the bar with Joe Gamble. Neither of them turned his head or appeared to notice Bolt. Walking to a table in the rear,

Bolt picked up a greasy deck of cards and began thumbing through them, laying out a game of solitaire.

Common sense, as well as a certain inner and deep-laid panic, warned him to run, to grab a horse and go, to get as far away from this country as possible. His little world was falling about his ears, and all because of two men. One, actually; for without the arrival of Hopalong Cassidy, Red Connors would now be dead and forgotten. One man.

He threw down the cards and got up in disgust and walked to the bar. "Rye!" he snapped, slapping his hand flat upon the bar. He was suddenly filled with ugly rage. "Rye, damn it!"

The bartender complied, avoiding his eyes. Jack Bolt downed the drink and took another, then turned and slammed through the twin doors. Joe Gamble looked after him.

"Mad," he said shortly. "What's he got to be mad about?"

"He'll have plenty if we get the deadwood on him," Monaghan said. "If I knew for sure that he was the rustler, I'd—"

"You'd better get ready, then. He's our man." Gamble looked at his own drink. "Hoppy sent a wire off somewhere, and unless I'm much mistaken, when he gets an answer things are going to pop. Red Connors did some prospectin' out there, and I figure he got the proof, or something anyway. Those two hombres could trail a snake through a thick fog, believe me."

Jack Bolt stood on the boardwalk in the sunlight. He stared one way and then another. All eyes avoided him. More than anything else this told him his stack of chips had run out and he was down to the boards. He spat viciously and stared fiercely at a man sitting on the boardwalk. He felt like kicking the man, like striking him, killing him. And he did not even know him.

Striding down the walk, his boot steps rang hard on the boards, but no head turned. It was like being dead, as if he moved through a world where he could not be seen. Already the story had gone the rounds. And people believed him a rustler. All right! Let them believe it! He'd show them! Cassidy had been the cause of his misfortunes, so Cassidy would die!

Griffin! Why, that poor, egotistical fool! To believe he could kill a man like Hopalong! To kill such a man you had to plan carefully or take a great chance. You could never do it in the haphazard way Pod Griffin had tried it. Nor could you do it from too great a distance.

Jack Bolt stopped suddenly, his eyes straying up and down the street, his brain suddenly sharp with calculation. That upstairs window over the bank—it had been an office, but the lawyer had left town. It was empty now. A man up there with a rifle . . . He nodded to himself. That was it.

But why take a chance on just one man? A man there with a rifle, but another up the street in the loft of the livery stable. Another on the bluff over the town. Swiftly he chose his positions and considered the situation. It was all or nothing now. He would have to hit hard and suddenly. He must kill so completely and wipe out his enemies so well that never again would a hand be lifted against him in this town.

Suppose—just suppose he could get Connors, Cassidy, Monaghan, and Gamble all at once? Then ride on to the 3TL and take care of Gibson and Gillespie? Suppose he could catch them in the street, down them quickly? Suppose a message was delivered to them by some stranger, somebody who would call them all together in plain view of his unseen marksmen? A volley of shots—and then he could appear and be all sorrow and sadness.

Sim Aragon would soon be in town, and with him would be Pete and some of the boys. It would be enough. Once the leaders were dead, the others could suspect all they wanted to! Let them suspect; it would put fear in them, destroy their ability to organize against him.

Passing Manuel on the street, he whispered, "At the bar down by the creek, in two hours. Get Sim."

CHAPTER 19

Hoppy Grows Suspicious

Hopalong Cassidy walked into the restaurant and sat down. Red Connors strolled after him and seated himself nearby, where he could keep an eye on the back door to the kitchen. Whatever was going to happen would happen tonight. And if Jack Bolt suspected they were pinning this on him, he would be sure to start something.

Hopalong stretched his legs under the table and reached for the egg- and coffee-stained menu, which was written on the back of an old show-card advertising *East Lynne.* His eyes looked over it at the street. Bolt was standing on a corner as if deep in thought.

Dru Monaghan came in—a tall, grim-looking man, neat in cattleman's clothes, looking every inch the rancher. He nodded at Hopalong and dropped into a chair. Joe Gamble joined him, and the four men were silent.

"Grub's good here," Red said finally. "Be a relief to get away from my own cookin'."

"Your cooking?" Hopalong chuckled. "Joe did all the cooking. You couldn't boil the hide off a steer!"

"Huh! You talk about your own cookin', not mine." Red

eyed the back door suspiciously. Bolt was a little too obvious out there on the corner.

"How long will it take to hear from that sheriff?" Monaghan wanted to know.

Hopalong shrugged. "Maybe a few hours, maybe a few days. It's hard to tell. The message doesn't go straight through. It has to be re-sent a couple of times. There may be delays."

"Hope Bolt won't leave town."

"He won't."

Jack Bolt waited in the shade of a store awning and watched the street. A buckboard drawn by a pair of half-broken mustangs clattered and rattled down the street, and then a heavy freighter's wagon, drawn by a long string of mules. A barefooted boy walked by with a stick in his hand and a nondescript dog at his side. After a while Grat and Bones turned the corner near the livery stable and started towards him. Again his eyes surveyed the street. Slim was down at the Picket Pin, a small bar just around the corner and off the one street of the town.

The Picket Pin had long been a hangout for his boys. It faced the creek and a row of huge old cottonwoods. Beyond the creek, which was shallow, gravel-bottomed, and only about six feet wide, was a corral where several of the townspeople held their saddle horses. Probably the Breed was down there, too. A showdown was coming, and they all knew it.

Grat swung down from his horse, a big, rough-dressed man, hard-bitten and tough. He had acquired new respect for his boss since the killing of Pod Griffin. How fast Griffin had been, Grat did not know, although he had always talked a good fight—but one thing he did understand and no mistake about it. The boss was much, much faster.

"What's up, boss?" he asked. "Anything doin'?"

"There will be." Bolt looked up at him, then over at Bones. "See Slim and the Breed and tell them to stay close to the Picket Pin. Cassidy's in town."

Grat's mouth opened to speak, then closed. Cassidy was not dead. Pod had been mistaken. Grat's jaw set hard. That silly fool! Couldn't he do anything right? Grat turned impatiently and strode down the street, and after a moment's hesitation Bones followed.

Hopalong Cassidy alive! Grat did not like it. He liked no part of it. And Red Connors, too. He recalled his own conversation with Cassidy on the trail when they were chasing Red. He had warned Cassidy then of what he would do if he saw him around again. Did Hopalong recall that warning? Grat hoped not. He was a fighter, but he wanted no shootouts with a man of that caliber. Life was short enough, and if by some miracle he should beat Hopalong, like as not he would only be downed by some half-smart kid with a desire for a reputation. Like Pod Griffin.

Grat's cigarette suddenly tasted bad, and he hurled it into the dust. Then he turned the corner and pushed into the Picket Pin. The interior was cool and dark. Slim sat at a table playing cards with Manuel Aragon and two other men, both Aragon riders. The Breed stood at the bar, drinking. Grat walked up beside him. "Go easy on that stuff," he warned. "Bolt won't like it."

The Breed turned his yellowish eyes on Grat. He smiled, and his teeth were even and white. He had beautiful teeth, but there was nothing else beautiful about him. His boots were down at the heel and long unpolished. His trousers were stained and soiled. A stubble of hairs grew on his chin and upper lip—thick hairs that he shaved once every few weeks. Grat could see that telling the Breed to stop now would be a waste of time. Grat called for a drink and felt Bones take his place alongside him. Suddenly Grat was impatient with Bones. The man was his shadow. He was never without him, he—

"Grat!"

He turned to see that Bolt had come into the room and was motioning to him. Grat tossed off his drink and crossed to the table. Then Bolt called to Bones and the Breed. Manuel Aragon moved over, and Sim suddenly walked into the room from the rear. One of the men with Manuel got up from the table and walked to the door, where he sat down on a bench from which he could see anyone who approached.

A half hour later, when Grat left the Picket Pin, it was to walk towards the livery barn. He went up the street first and mounted his horse, riding it to a place in the shade of the stable, where he could reach it easily. Careful that he was not seen, Grat slipped his rifle from the scabbard and, entering the livery stable, climbed to the loft. Once there, he bellied down in the hay to the left of the wide second-floor door, through which hay was thrown into the loft. From this point he could cover all the far side of the street and most of the street itself. He jacked a shell into the chamber. The payoff was coming, and he was relieved. He hoped it would not be long. His mouth was already dry.

In the deserted office above the bank Manuel Aragon placed his rifle carefully beside the window. Grat was in the stable, and what Grat could not see of the street Manuel could. In another window of the same office was Slim, with a Spencer 56.

Bones plodded up behind the building and walked to the

back of the hardware store. He left his horse there in the mouth of the draw that opened to the hills beyond. He had the best getaway of them all, the very best. But he would have to take his place behind some rubbish at the rear of the store.

From there he could prevent anyone taking shelter in the space between the saloon and the hardware store and could see a part of the street. Other men were carefully disposed about town so that no getaway would be possible. Caught by fire in the middle of the street, their instinctive action would be a jump for shelter in a gap between buildings. And now a rifleman covered each gap, ready for just such a move.

Jack Bolt considered his situation and the dispersal of his men. Four rifles would cover the group in the street, and they would open fire simultaneously. If their guns did not get the men they sought, some of the other ambushing riflemen would. And with that lot out of the way the countryside would be in the hands of Bolt and the Aragons. The few remaining, like Gibson, could be taken care of very easily.

Suddenly Bolt's spirits rose. This was a time when Hopalong could not get away. He was closed in from every approach, as were the others. For Hopalong alone was not enough now. This had to be sudden, terrifying, and complete. Hopalong Cassidy, Red Connors, Joe Gamble, and Dru Monaghan were the four marked for murder.

Jack Bolt walked slowly down the street towards the saloon. There was no sense waiting. He would get this started now. And if any of them should try to get back into the saloon he would, if necessary, take care of them himself. The messenger should arrive within the half hour, and that would be the end. He stepped into the saloon and sauntered across to the bar.

Hopalong Cassidy had walked over from the restaurant and was seated at a table with Red Connors. He looked up as Bolt walked in. Instantly he was alert. Every line of the man exuded confidence and readiness. Red's eyes followed Hopalong's.

"Now what's got into him?" Red demanded. "He looks like he's the cat that's been eatin' the canaries."

Hopalong got to his feet. "Trouble coming—I can smell it. That hombre has got something up his sleeve."

Dru Monaghan and Joe Gamble looked at the two men curiously. "What is it? What do you think?"

"What would please him most?"

"Most? Why, to see the four of us dead," Monaghan suggested. "Why?"

"Then we'd better look sharp," Hopalong replied dryly. "He looks mighty happy to me!"

CHAPTER 20

Cold-blooded Killing

Despite the tension, night drew near without any break in the ordered calm of the day. Men drifted reluctantly home, and others went to the saloon and stood along the bar, drinking a little, talking, and listening. Rumors were still rife, and it was noticed that neither Hopalong Cassidy nor Red Connors showed any evidence of leaving town. Moreover, about dusk Frank Gillespie rode in and stripped the saddle from his horse. With him was a well-set-up young man with cold gray eyes. He was dressed in almost-new clothes that seemed to have been carefully brushed only minutes before.

"You think Cassidy is dead, then?"

Gillespie shrugged. "All I know is the rumor. You can't keep a thing like that quiet. Anyway, what I hear now came to me from a 4H cowhand. He heard it from somebody else. This Pod Griffin killed Hopalong and was killed later by his own boss, Jack Bolt."

"Bolt a friend of Cassidy's?"

"Not so's you'd know it. Bolt is ramroddin' that rustler outfit or I miss my guess. He killed Pod because he got too big for his breeches, that's all."

Gillespie looked at the stranger again. They had met on

the trail, and he was beginning to realize that he had done all the talking himself. He knew no more about this man now than when they had met. Nevertheless there was something about him he liked, although the two tied-down guns spoke of a man who understood trouble.

Simply and directly as possible he explained the situation as it now stood in the country around Tascotal, ending with the return of the cattle and the capture of Cardoza and the cook. Then he added, "About sundown I took a *pasear* aroun' the hills near our range. Some distance off I spotted a party of riders. I didn't have no glasses with me, but I spotted a horse I knowed. It was Sim Aragon's."

"Headed for town?"

"Uh-huh. Well, I knowed that Monaghan and Gamble had come in here, and that Red Connors would come to town if he was alive, so I figured the big payoff was due. I grabbed my rifle and headed on over."

"Good man. I'm in this, too."

Gillespie searched the young man's face. "How's that? I don't place you."

"Why, I was down country, sort of ambulatin' this way, when I heard a rumor that Cassidy was in a knock-down and drag-out range war, so I hit the trail for Tascotal. Hoppy's a friend of mine. My name's Jenkins. Mesquite Jenkins."

Frank Gillespie stared. This, then, was the holy terror of whom Red had talked almost as much as he had talked of Hopalong! He swallowed.

"Say! That's great!" An idea occurred to him. "Look, nobody here knows you. I'll take a look around town, and we'll meet back here in an hour if nothin' starts. All right?"

Mesquite nodded. "Where does this outfit hang out?"

"Right around that corner. Place called the Picket Pin. Better watch your step if you go there."

"I'll watch it. Back here, in an hour."

Mesquite Jenkins turned swiftly towards the Picket Pin. He had arrived too late to help Hopalong, but not too late to settle the crowd that had done him in. If Red was in town—all right, the two of them would go through this bunch like soup through a tall Swede. He sauntered around the corner and met the eye of the man on the bench. He kept going, and the man stood up.

"Goin' somewhere?" The watchman was elaborately casual.

"Inside," Mesquite said briefly, "for a drink. They sell it, don't they?"

"Sure, but right now there's folks busy inside."

"I reckon the door still opens both ways. All your saloons keep a sentry outside? Or is that a special courtesy?"

The outlaw's face darkened. He decided he did not like this cold-faced youngster. It might be a good time to teach him a lesson.

"It's special," he said. "Now beat it!"

Mesquite Jenkins had long been a disciple of the idea that once the point of battle is reached, no good can result from continued conversation or argument. The guard had told him what to do. He turned on his heel with a shrug, but suddenly, as he turned, his right hand shot up, grasped the man's rifle by the middle, and shoved. The guard staggered, the bench caught him behind the knees, and his heels flew up, his head down. His head tunked dully on the butt end of a log, and the guard blanked out.

Jenkins picked up the rifle and shucked the shells from it,

then tossed them away. Shoving open the door, he strode into the saloon and to the bar.

Sim Aragon looked up angrily. Most of his men were already placed, but he did not relish interruptions. Nevertheless the man was a stranger and he walked to the bar without apparent interest. Two or three habitués of the place loafed there in low-voiced conversation, so Sim ignored the visitor.

Mesquite remained at the bar for several minutes, and in those minutes he heard several interesting things. Leaving his drink unfinished, Mesquite walked out. The first thing he saw was the guard struggling to his feet. Calmly Mesquite hung a pistol barrel over his skull and walked on. What he had heard was important. Hopalong Cassidy was alive. He was with Red at the saloon in the hotel. And something was in the wind.

Jack Bolt had made his own decision after seeing Cassidy and the others. He had decided suddenly to stop his messenger and to let the whole thing ride until morning. In the bright morning sunlight, when men were relieved of the fears of the night, the messenger could arrive and they would believe the rustlers had struck again, elsewhere. It was the best plan. And when the four men congregated in the street there would be an end to it.

Among the things he did not count upon was a cat-footed young man who watched Manuel Aragon come down the back stairs of the bank building and steal softly away. That same young man saw Bones rise from behind a rubbish pile and begin idly working over his harness. Mesquite nodded grimly. The attack had been called off. He would avoid his friends and stay on the outskirts to watch.

The hours of darkness marched solemnly past, like groups of dark-robed monks proceeding to a morning mass. A few desultory card games whiled the evening away, and a few loiterers lingered long at the bars, but nothing broke the stillness of the evening; the night was serene, starlit, and cool.

At the Picket Pin only a few men gathered. Others came and went about their various activities, having a drink, speaking in low-voiced conversation with each other, hearing guarded messages from the bartender or Bolt himself, then drifting out again.

Only one thing happened during the night, and that not discovered until daybreak. It was the operator at the telegraph station who discovered it—a man was murdered.

Old Dave Wills had been the town's handyman for longer than most people could remember. He worked at odd jobs, and his one steady task was handling freight at the railroad station. He had been in the station's freight-storage room when the operator closed up. He was still there, dead from a knife wound, when he was found. The weapon had been carried away. Nothing was missing.

It had been after midnight when Jack Bolt decided to see what was in the message or messages sent by Hopalong Cassidy. The greater part of Tascotal was in darkness, and Bolt slipped quietly from his room and down the back alleys of the town towards the station. Behind the hardware store he thought he detected a shadow, but a fifteen-minute wait developed nothing, so he went on, determined not to be seen even if he failed in his effort.

The station was fifty yards from the nearest building, and

across the tracks were the stockyards from which cattle were shipped. From the last building in the street he made a short dash to a blasted boulder, removed from the right of way when the railroad was put through. Then he moved forward in the low shadow of the railroad grade.

The station platform was dark and still, but opening a window was a small task for one so long expert in crime. Inside, he hastily rifled through the stack of messages. There were not many, most of them having to do with shipments or invoices of freight received. Suddenly he stopped.

> JACK BRONSON REPORTED BUYING STOCK IN WYOMING AND NE-
> VADA. MET HERD OUTSIDE GOOSE LAKE. BRANDS CHECK WITH
> YOUR MESSAGE. HOLDING CATTLE AND HANDS FOR INVESTIGA-
> TION.
>
> GEORGE CUYLER,
> SHERIFF.

Jack Bolt stared at the message as if hoping the words would change before his eyes, but they did not. This was worse, much worse, than he had expected! This was the end, then. His dream of having a ranch and security, of having a vast herd of his own—it was all at an end.

Alone in the dark room, long after his match went out, he stood there holding the message in his hands. Then he struck another match and shifted the page. Beneath it lay another.

> ANSWERS DESCRIPTION OF MOBEETIE JACK BIRCHEN, WANTED
> HERE FOR RUSTLING, MURDER, AND STAGE ROBBERY. HOLD FOR
> INVESTIGATION.
>
> JONES, MAJOR,
> TEXAS RANGERS.

A sudden movement startled him, and he glanced up. Old Dave stood in the doorway to the storage room where he slept.

"Who's there? What do you want?"

The old man came on into the room, striking a match. "Oh? It's you, Mr. Bolt? Why, I'd— Uh, uh-h-h." Writhing, the old man sank to the floor. The hard-driven knife had gone deep. Bitterly Bolt stared down at him.

"You old fool!" he snarled. "Why didn't you stay where you belonged?"

Returning the messages to the pigeonhole, he slipped out the window and returned to his room. Now, more than ever, only one thing remained. To kill Cassidy and get out of the country, and fast.

He paused an instant, undressing. Those messages! They had not been delivered! Surely, if they had been, Hopalong would already have been after him. Yet the ones he had seen were copies—the real messages must be at the hotel and somehow had not yet come into Hopalong's hands! For an instant he was moved to go at once and try to get ahold of them, but that was useless. Cuyler would be checking soon, and would wire again. He would have to destroy the copies as well, and he was glad he had not done so, for they would have been a clue to the new killing—that of Dave Wills.

Dawn found him wide awake, but tired. He had slept, but he had not rested. He stared up the street, his hatred a living, breathing thing within him. "All right, you fool!" He muttered the words half aloud. "You'll get yours within the next couple of hours, and when you do, it will be good!"

He dressed hurriedly and went at once to the Picket Pin.

·   ·   ·

Hopalong Cassidy awakened from a sound sleep to find the messages tucked under his door. After they had arrived the night before, Dave Wills had taken them to deliver, but had wandered off on business of his own and had only delivered the messages after Hopalong was asleep. Once he had read them, Hopalong woke Red Connors.

"There it is," he said quietly. "We've got all we want. We'll go down the street and pick him up this morning, if he's still in town—and if he's not, we'll go find him."

Dru Monaghan came across the hall at the sound of their voices and read the messages. "Well, you hit it right, Cassidy," he admitted. "There's no doubt now. Joe an' I'll go along."

"Don't forget about last night!" Red warned. "That Bolt looked too sure of hisself to suit me! We've got to look sharp! He won't quit without a showdown, you can bet on that!"

Hopalong nodded without speaking. Before falling asleep he had studied the situation carefully. That the showdown would come today he knew, and putting himself in the place of Jack Bolt—or Bronson, or Birchen, or whatever his name was —he tried to decide what the man would do. He knew that more than one of the Aragon outfit was in town. He also knew that Grat, Bones, and others of the 8 Boxed H were here also. With such an outfit of hard cases they could put up quite a battle.

Bolt knew where Cassidy was. Bolt would know that a showdown must come, and about how it must begin. Hence, Bolt would attempt an ambush or a trap of some kind.

CHAPTER 21

Whizzing Lead!

"**N**o use going off half-cocked," Cassidy suggested, smiling. "Let's eat breakfast. I could use some of those hen eggs that gent downstairs serves up."

"Eggs!" Red shook his head. "Why, I can recall when there wasn't an egg to be found west of the Pecos. Everybody ate beef three times a day!"

"My mother brought three hens an' a rooster across the plains," Dru said. "I was only knee-high to a tall ox about that time, an' she had me shakin' the seeds of every plant we came to for chicken feed. She set powerful store by those chickens."

Hopalong had drifted to the back door of the kitchen when the others sat down. He looked out into the yard from either side of the door. It looked bright, sunny, and beautiful. He was not deceived. That such a place could harbor danger he knew well.

The rubbish pile held his attention. A man concealed there could cover not only the backs of the buildings but the passage between the hardware store and the saloon that adjoined the hotel and dining room. Opening the door carefully, Hopalong stepped out. It took him only a minute to ascertain there was no one behind the rubbish pile, but the print of a pair of toes and knees was all too plain. Someone had been kneeling there the previous night! This, then, was one of their lookouts, one of the places they could expect a gunman.

As he was turning away he saw something else—the print of a pair of almost-new boots worn by a man with small feet. Something about those prints struck a responsive chord, but the boots were so new as to offer almost no clue to their wearer. Apparently their wearer had been scouting the position just as he was. Puzzled, he went back inside.

He missed Bones by a few minutes only, for the fat outlaw was even at that moment checking his rifle at the livery stable preparatory to returning to his position.

Hopalong Cassidy returned to his seat at the table as the eggs were served. Red Connors grinned at him.

"Home was never like this!" he said. "How many times I've followed a herd over the trail when I would have given my saddle for just one egg. Just anythin' but beef and beans!"

"And I've seen it when you'd have given your saddle for beef and beans," Hopalong said, smiling. "And so would I, many a time."

"You reckon they'll still be in town?" Gamble asked suddenly.

"Sure," Cassidy replied. "They've something up their sleeves. There's too many of them here."

"Where's Sue?" Red asked. "Did she start back?"

"Saw her in the hall. She'll be down in a few minutes," Dru told them. "It would be better if she had gone back."

A buckboard rattled by in the street, and then suddenly, from up the street toward the station, there was a wild yell. The operator rushed down the street and charged into the hotel dining room. "Wills is dead!" he said. "Somebody busted into the station last night and murdered him."

Swiftly a crowd circled the station agent. Monaghan scowled. "Now, why would anybody murder an old codger like him? Or for that matter, why would anybody bust into the station?"

Connors looked over at Cassidy, and Hopalong nodded. "Could be. It could be that somebody heard I'd sent some messages and got curious. The old man might have interrupted whoever broke in and got killed for his pains."

"Not much use to kill him, seems to me. The whole story was in those messages."

"Unless Dave wanted to hold him," Monaghan suggested, "or the hombre lost his head."

A hard-ridden horse swung down the street and skidded to a stop before the hotel. A rider hit the dust and burst inside. "Cassidy!" he yelled. "Outlaws hittin' the 3TL! Must be a dozen of 'em! I was comin' by an' seen 'em. They shot at me! Gillespie looks like he's standin' 'em off, but he can't hold out for long."

The rider jumped for the door and was gone as the four men lunged to their feet and rushed for the street, grabbing their rifles as they went. Hopalong vaulted the fence and rushed for the livery stable just as a wild Texas yell rang out above the town, and then two guns bellowed as one.

A bullet whipped by Hopalong's cheek and he spun on his heel. Before him gaped the opening between the hardware store and the hotel, and at the far end the pile of rubbish. Instantly he saw it all. The shouted warning of the attack, the rush into the street . . . Guns were bellowing, and he saw Joe Gamble hit the ground in a heap, his face contorted. Hopalong took a jump for the bank building and flattened against the wall. Somebody on a roof was firing with a rifle, but not at him.

He glanced again at the rubbish pile, then deliberately rounded the corner of the bank and started for the stair. The shot that missed him had come from the second floor. He went up fast, seeing Red Connors down behind a water trough and Dru Monaghan, wounded and staggering, heading for the Emporium.

A bullet smacked the rock of the bank wall before him and spat angry flakes in his face before it whined away into the distance. Another bullet hit and then another. He felt something hit the step under his feet, and then he lunged through the door. A bullet broke the window behind him, and he flattened against the wall. At least one rifleman was here, on this almost deserted second floor of the bank, and that man he intended to get.

Outside, bullets still sounded in the street. Wheeling, he lifted the rifle and let three fast shots go at the top door in the livery barn. Then, placing his rifle against the doorjamb, he yanked out a six-gun and turned towards the hallway.

Here all was still. The sounds outside seemed far away. Then he heard the harsh bark of a gun from the room near him, and heard feet scuff on the floor. Did the unknown outlaw know Cassidy was here? Was he waiting for him even now?

Sweat trickled down Cassidy's cheek. He listened, his ears attuned to the slightest sound. The seconds passed like hours, and he moved on tiptoe, fighting for silence, towards the hall door. It opened gently under his hand, then creaked. He froze in place, the doorknob in one hand, his gun in the other.

No sound.

The room smelled faintly musty, and the air was close, as of a place long shut away from air and movement. There was dust on the floor. The rifle in the next room barked again, and an answering shot tinkled glass. Hopalong eased himself into the hallway and stood waiting with poised gun. The shooting outside had now become scattered. Obviously, the various fighters were taking their places and getting set for a long battle.

The hall was long, and four doors opened off it on either side. At either end was a window, but only one stairway led to this floor—the one up which he had come.

Wind stirred and the door behind him creaked slightly. Hopalong watched the other doors with careful eyes, then moved forward. The rifle barked again, and he selected the door and made two hurried steps before he paused to listen again. The door was one step farther. Glancing swiftly down the hall, he thought he saw a knob move slightly and he waited, but hearing movement within the room where the rifleman was, he looked around again, then stepped quickly across and threw the door open.

Manuel Aragon spun on his heel, dropping his rifle and grabbing for his Colt.

"Drop it!" Hopalong yelled.

Aragon snarled and his fingers closed on the gun butt. Behind Hopalong the door creaked, and he fired as Manuel jerked to lift his gun. The bullet hit Aragon and turned him halfway round, and instantly Hopalong wheeled, dropping to one knee. A dark figure loomed before him, bearded and wild. The man held a gun, a big Walker Colt, and both weapons flamed as one. Hopalong felt the shock of the bullet and heard a second report as he fired, a report that was not his own. His shot missed as the shock of the bearded man's bullet turned him. Instantly he steadied and fired again, and the bearded man pitched forward on his face, mouthing curses.

Glancing down, Hopalong saw that the man's bullet had hit his cartridge belt and had fired one of his own shells. There was a bloody tear in his jeans where the bullet had ripped its way down, burying itself in the floor. Manuel Aragon lay sprawled out on the floor, and Hopalong sprang across to him, seeing the movement of his lungs that betrayed the fact that he lived. Picking up both six-gun and rifle, Hopalong hurled them through the window, then did the same with the bearded man's weapons. Outside there was more shooting, and he rushed for the door. Instantly a shot rang out and a bullet cut through the door within inches of his reaching hand.

Another bullet holed the door higher up. No chance to get out here. Wheeling, he ran down the hall to the back window, knowing the front must be under cover of a half-dozen rifles. The back window opened on a shed roof, and Hopalong took a quick look and stepped out. He had holstered his .45 and now carried the Winchester. Suddenly, not a block away, a man skylined himself on a rooftop and shot. Hopalong's rifle came up, but he held his fire. The man was shooting at something in the street. There was something familiar about that man on the roof, something Hopalong could not quite place.

Dropping from the roof of the shed, Hopalong turned towards the street. Instantly a shot grooved the wood within an inch of his face. He sprang back, then circled towards the far side of the bank. At the corner he faced a street empty except for the body of Joe Gamble, who lay sprawled there. Dru Monaghan was nowhere in sight, nor was Red Connors.

Hopalong dropped his rifle suddenly and sprinted for the far side of the street. A bullet clipped past his head, another kicked up dust just short of him, and then with a long dive he hit the street rolling and ended up against the boardwalk. A bullet slammed the walk over his head, and he realized he was in an absolutely impossible position. Yet to rise meant death.

He turned his head and saw that the walk itself was raised about eight or nine inches from the ground at this point, and beyond it he could see the litter of bottles and refuse under the saloon. Edging under the walk, he crawled back under the saloon proper. Here there were at least two feet of clearance. Grasping his six-guns to assure himself that he had not lost them under the walk, he crawled towards the back of the hotel. After a quick look he crawled out and straightened up.

The rubbish pile was unchanged, but behind it lay the sprawled body of Bones. The fat outlaw was dead. A bullet had struck him over the ear and ranged downwards through his skull. Evidently, the rifleman Cassidy had seen upon the roof. Hopalong opened the back door of the saloon and stepped in.

Two men were standing inside the front door, and both were armed. The bartender, his face pale, was standing near the bar, his shoulder trickling blood.

"Look out!" he whispered. "That's Sim Aragon!" At the sound both men turned. The three men faced each other across the saloon. Sim Aragon smiled with thin, scarred lips. "So? This is Hopalong Cassidy? I have looked for you, *amigo.*"

"You've found me," Hopalong replied shortly.

Aragon's hand dropped, and Hopalong's guns leaped from his holsters, blasting fire. Sim Aragon dropped his gun and spun, buckling at the knees. Then he fell, striking the man beside him and throwing him off balance. Hopalong held his fire.

"Don't try it!" he warned. "Drop your gun!"

Pete Aragon glared. "You've killed my brother!"

"He asked for it. Drop your guns!"

For an instant Aragon hesitated. With a shrug he moved his hands carefully to his buckle and let go his belt. Then he stepped away. His black eyes never left Hopalong. "Can I look at him? Maybe he is not dead."

"Go ahead—only don't get any ideas."

There was silence in the streets. Then, some distance away, a door slammed and there was a murmur of voices. Reassured by the end of the shooting, people were coming out into the streets. Red Connors was the first one through the door. His shirt was ripped and bloody.

"I ain't hurt," he protested as he saw Hopalong's eyes. "Just split the hide and ruined my shirt."

The door swung open, and both men looked around. In the door, grinning, was Mesquite Jenkins!

"Where did you spring from?" Hopalong demanded.

"Heard you were up here, so I headed north. When I found out about this trouble I figured I could learn more and do more by bein' where I wasn't known, so I stayed away from you."

"Where's Dru, Red? Was he hurt?"

"He caught two slugs, but he'll live. Fact is, he was still on his feet when last I saw him. Gamble's not dead either. He's got him a broken leg and a slug through the shoulder, though."

"How about them?"

"I don't know. Let's see."

They started for the door, and Mesquite commented on Bones: "I spotted that place right off. He was holed up there where he could kill any one who jumped between the buildings for shelter. They had 'em all laid out right to get you, Hoppy."

Bones was dead. Manuel Aragon and the bearded outlaw were both living, but the bearded outlaw was in very bad shape. Manuel Aragon stared at Hopalong with hard eyes.

"Some day," he muttered through lips twisted with pain, "I keel you!"

Four outlaws had been killed, three were badly wounded, two more slightly wounded. Pete Aragon had surrendered.

Of Jack Bolt and Grat there was no sign.

CHAPTER 22

Unfinished Business

It was plain that Red Connors was disgusted by the news.

"Got clean away," Red Connors said bitterly. "And Bolt won't head for California, because he knows the sheriff will be waiting for him there."

"It looks to me," Hopalong replied slowly, "like the smart thing to do would be to ride out to the 8 Boxed H and give the place a going over. We might find something there that would tip us off."

Mesquite Jenkins suddenly scowled. "Say, where's that other hombre? He said he worked for the 3TL. Tall, high cheekbones, brown hair."

"Sounds like Gillespie." Connors looked questioningly at Mesquite. "Where'd you know him?"

"Rode into town with him. We were going to meet at the corral, but I was late and he wasn't there. Come to think of it, I think Gillespie was the name."

"Let's have a look." Hastily the three men got to their feet and started for the door. Outside, people were gathered about in knots, talking and arguing. All eyes turned to the three, and although many admiring, interested glances went their way, there were a few that were hostile.

Despite their questions, they could find no one who had seen the 3TL hand. At the livery stable the man who had lent the palouse to Hopalong nodded to their question.

"Saw him last night," he said. "He slept here. He was prowlin' around most of the night, ugly as a grizzly with a sore paw. One thing I do know—he was some interested in Jack Bolt."

Cassidy considered this, his eyes thoughtful. Shoving his hat back on his head, he dropped to his heels, chewing on a bit of hay. As he turned the situation over in his mind it began to clarify, in some respects at least. There was every chance that Gillespie had been most interested in Bolt. That he disliked the outlaw rancher he had already shown, and that he did not trust him. Their words of the day after the herd was recovered returned to mind. Gillespie was almost sure to concentrate on Bolt, of all the outlaws. The lean Scot was a stubborn man, and not one to relinquish a fight without adequate reason.

"I've a hunch," Hopalong suggested, "that when we find Gillespie, our man Bolt won't be far away. Chances are he followed Bolt and Grat when they slipped out of town."

"Where would they go?" Red said irritably. "No use him going to the 8 Boxed H, and he would expect us to look there and at the 3TL. Anyway, he could gain nothing by going there. The 4H is watching for him, and so's the 3F. Whatever he has done, he's flown the coop."

"He knows that country west of here," Hopalong said.

"He knows it north, too." The liveryman looked up. "I know he does because he used to come in here and hire horses from me to ride that way."

"He tell you that was where he went?"

"No, Cassidy, he sure didn't, but I don't need to be told. Except in the Pine Forests, there's no timber west of here, and from the needles I used to comb out of those horses' tails, he went through thick timber. There's timber northeast of here along the state line. And the fact is, that's the only way he could have gone in the time he had."

"Had he hired any horses lately?" Hopalong asked.

"No, not just lately. The last time was almost two months ago, but before that he was ridin' that way right reg'lar. Two, three times a week. Carried some grub with him, I think."

Studying the matter, Hopalong looked up at Mesquite. "How about you walkin' over to the Emporium and asking a few questions? Red, drop in at the hardware store. See if Bolt bought any tools or other gear there, say a couple or three months back."

When they had gone Hopalong considered the matter further. "Did he ever take a pack horse?"

"Not that I know of. He had some sizable packs behind his saddle nearly every time, though."

"If a man rode north, where would he be apt to go?" Hopalong asked. "I don't know that country up there."

The liveryman shrugged. "There ain't no place to go. Just range country, then some mountains and some scattered timber. There isn't a ranch or even a prospector's cabin anywhere to the north."

He chewed a moment, then spat. "Tell you, though. You go by way of Agate. It's out of your way a mite, but you talk to Sourdough. It seems to me he prospected that country a few years back."

Red was coming back, walking rapidly, and Mesquite was coming from the other direction. Red was grinning. "Now what do you know?" he exclaimed. "You can sure read your sign,

Hoppy! About three months back Bolt started buyin' supplies. The stuff for his ranch always went out of here in a buckboard, but not this. He had sacks made up to tote behind his saddle, but not like a man would carry for an overnight or two-day camp. It was like he was layin' in a stock."

Mesquite nodded, his eyes bright with grim satisfaction. "That fits! About three, maybe four months ago Jack Bolt bought a hammer and some nails. Graves back there figured it was funny, because they had bought a big stock at the ranch not long before. Then he came in later and bought an axe, a shovel, and a pick. That was on the last day of March. Graves set it down in a book because he had to order some axes, that being his last one.

"Three weeks later Bolt came in and bought some hinges and a hasp, then a heavy padlock."

"He could have used all that at his ranch," Red said dubiously.

The liveryman nodded. "He could've, but I doubt it."

"I'm betting he didn't!" Mesquite replied shortly. "I'm betting Bolt played it safe. He built himself a cabin somewhere and stocked it with grub. Isn't that right, Hoppy?"

Hopalong Cassidy nodded. "Bolt is a careful operator. It was only the fact that Red stumbled on some suspicious tracks that started all this trouble. Otherwise he might have gotten away with what he was doing. I think that Bolt was playing it very safe and had another hideout located if he needed it. Something he didn't even want his own men to know about."

"Makes sense, I guess," Red agreed. "But how're we goin' to find it?"

"He'd want water," Mesquite mused, "and, unless I miss my guess, a lookout from where he could keep an eye on his back trail. He might not care about that, but I've an idea he would."

"Water, fuel, and shelter. With the tools he got he could build a shelter, yet he would have to have a place in which to build it."

Hopalong turned to the liveryman. "About a horse, now," he suggested. "Do you remember any time when Bolt had more than one horse? Or did he buy a horse from you at any time? My idea is that he would want an extra horse up there. Maybe a couple of them."

"No." The liveryman was positive. "He didn't buy any horse in this town, or I'd have heard of it. But he might have picked one up anywhere. There's an hombre over north of Paradise who runs a few horses. Folks say he does a right smart business with strangers who need horses in a hurry."

"We'll look him up," Hopalong said, rising.

"Better go it with a loose gun," the liveryman replied dryly. "He's reported unfriendly."

An hour later, assured that Joe Gamble was resting easily and that Monaghan was out of danger, the three riders saddled up and started back for the 3TL. They had gone no more than a mile when Sue Gibson overtook them. She flushed as she looked at Hopalong.

"I guess I was wrong about Jack Bolt," she said. "I've heard about those messages."

Cassidy smiled. "Forget it. I've been wrong a few times myself."

Red Connors snorted, and Mesquite's eyes twinkled. "Although," Cassidy continued, "not so wrong as some others I could name!"

"You were wrong when you didn't shoot down that no-account Griffin," Connors said flatly. "I knowed that for certain!"

Hopalong Cassidy rode into the 3TL ranch yard beside Sue Gibson, but as he swung down from the saddle Gibson himself limped from the house, smiling widely. Beside him was the man who had brought Topper back to Hopalong. Sighting him, the horse neighed shrilly, and Hoppy turned toward the corral. The horse ran eagerly to the gate and thrust his head over the bars.

"How are you, boy?" Hoppy ran his fingers under the white gelding's mane and scratched the horse's neck. "Good to be back, isn't it? How's the leg?"

Tapping the horse's foot gently, he lifted it and examined the leg. It looked as good as ever.

"We've got a trip to make, Topper. Let's go?" The horse jerked his head with pleasure at being back with Hopalong. Hopalong turned to Red as he walked up. "We'll stay here tonight, then start in the morning. We'll ride to Agate and talk to Sourdough. From there we'll probably have to check the trails north for tracks, but unless I miss my guess, this is one trail that will be hard to follow. He'll have no idea of letting anybody trace him."

Late the next day Sourdough told them what he could about the country. Then he added, "I ain't seen none of that crowd around town, but Hanson, who has him a little place down on the crick, lost a horse the other night. Lost a horse, a shoulder of beef, and some beans. Stole off him. Also about two dozen 56 Spencer shells."

"That might have been Slim," Red said. "I recall he had him a Spencer carbine."

The trail north led up the bottom of a wide canyon, its sides scattered with stubby timber and some undergrowth. There was no evidence of travel in a long time. They saw occasional deer, rabbits, and once a huge timber wolf who trotted unhurriedly off into the scrub growth on the mountainside.

"We'll just have to work north, check the streams and water holes, and watch all the trails," Hopalong told them. "It might be that Slim and the Breed know something, but I'm gambling they don't. I doubt if even Grat knew about this hang-out unless Bolt took him there."

"If there is a hideout!" Connors said. He scanned the mountainside and looked on ahead to where the valley narrowed. "What do you say we strike up the hill? We can see farther."

"Good idea!" Hoppy turned his horse around a boulder and started him up through the underbrush, mostly manzanita or tobacco bush. A grove of quaking aspen made a white-and-green arrow pointing up a slight hollow in the mountain. Curving around it, they rode on, keeping their eyes alert for movement or tracks.

The mountain sloped back and up, and they rode on, climbing steadily. Now the scattered growth thickened into clumps of alder and white-barked pine. Pausing under the shade of a red fir and its neighboring hemlock, Hopalong scanned the country. Suddenly he stood in his stirrups. "Fire," he said suddenly. "Out yonder."

Without a word they moved out, and when they had gone no more than half a mile Red Connors lifted his hand. "Here's a trail!" he called. "Two riders!"

Hopalong rode over. Neither track looked familiar now, but he would know them if he saw them again. Heading for the smoke once more, the three moved out. The tracks seemed to be going the same way.

"Must be an old camp," Mesquite suggested. "These tracks were made last night."

"Not by Bolt, I'll gamble!" Connors said flatly. "He'll play it smart from here on in!"

CHAPTER 23

Deadly Half-breed

$\mathbf{A}$dvancing with extreme care, the three spread out, working their way through the timber toward the thin blue line of smoke. Ahead, it climbed vaguely through the trees and lost itself against the sky. Finally they drew up. The smoke came from a hollow in the woods that was not far away among some boulders. Red circled, his rifle in his hands.

Hopalong advanced, following the tracks, then straightened in his stirrups to look over the bush toward the circle of the camp and the dying fire, but there was no sign of anyone around. Cautiously he closed in, his Winchester ready.

Two men had camped here—two men who could have been gone less than an hour. They had prepared and eaten a meal, but not much of one. Hopalong was standing by the charred remains of the fire when Red and Mesquite closed in.

"Gone," he said. "Maybe an hour ago, probably less. And they haven't much grub. They took the grounds out of the coffeepot."

Red prowled restlessly. "Two of them," he agreed. "It looks like the Breed and Slim."

"They saddled up in a hurry," Mesquite added, "and lit out like the devil was after 'em."

Cassidy nodded. "They must have spotted us back down the trail. All right." He gathered up his reins. "Let's get on after them."

They moved out swiftly, the trail plain to see. It went straight away into the scrub pine, then mounted a slope through saddle-high manzanita and wandered among some boulders. Twice they lost the trail, but each time Hopalong picked it up. Suddenly, far ahead, they sighted a rider.

"Take it easy," Hopalong said. "I think that hombre meant to be seen. Maybe the other one is lying along the trail somewhere."

They rode on. The day warmed and a slight breeze stirred the grass. Over the distant mountains thunderheads began to build their castles in the sky. The heat increased, the breeze died out, and the afternoon became sultry. They pushed on. Suddenly a rifle shot sounded and a bullet snarled past Hopalong's head. Red fired as if on signal and then dusted the clump of brush again. A horse's hoofs rattled on stone and were gone. The three pushed on, taking their time, aware that precipitate action could mean death.

The thunderheads built higher and turned darker, flattening out on the underside. Off in the far canyons thunder grumbled and muttered without humor. A gust of wind came and went. Another rifle shot sounded, but the marksman was too far away and they saw his bullet strike far ahead of them.

"Hot!" Connors mopped his face and neck, removing his hat to wipe off the band. "Sure is hot and sultry."

"It'll storm," Jenkins agreed.

"Wish I knew this country," Hopalong complained. "That storm is going to wipe out all the tracks."

"The answer to that is easy," Mesquite suggested. "Let's run 'em!"

"Not yet." Hopalong indicated their trail, the tracks wider-spaced now. "Let them do the running. They'll kill their horses if they don't stop soon."

Relentlessly the three riders pushed on. Sweat darkened the flanks and shoulders of their horses and the backs of their shirts. Time and again they wiped the hands that held their rifles. An hour passed, and then another. The mountain they were crossing spilled over into a deep green valley. A fresh bear track crossed the trail, and off to the left they saw a deer. Twice Hopalong pointed out tracks where horses had stumbled. The hunt was drawing to a close now. Once a bullet smashed through the branches over their heads, a feeling, tentative shot that lost itself in the forest.

Hesitating, to let the horses catch their breath, Hopalong voiced the thought that was troubling all of them. "The worst of it is, this isn't getting us any closer to Jack Bolt. He's the one we really want."

"It may be," Red said sullenly. "I was up this way the first week I was in this country. There's a valley north of here that runs east and west. We might be able to cut across country and then hunt for smoke. That's our best chance."

"There won't be any smoke," Mesquite objected. "Not if Bolt is smart." They were silent, agreeing. Jack Bolt would be found by no such obvious method.

The mountains grew taller, the canyons deeper and narrower. The growth along their flanks thickened, and the heat in the canyon bottoms was close and intense. Topper walked on tirelessly, seemingly untouched by the heat. Suddenly the narrow canyon up which they were riding ended against a dry waterfall, but over the rise on their right they could see an opening in the mountains. Cautiously they mounted the ridge. Before them was a low saddle, a gap in the hills that showed a beautiful green valley that might be three or four miles long and almost a half-mile wide.

Halfway down the valley was a log cabin and some crude pole corrals, and at the corral two men were dismounting. Hopalong leveled his glasses.

"That's it!" he said grimly. "But we'd better hurry. There's fresh horses in that corral!"

What happened then, they all saw. Riding down the gap, they plunged into the valley, pushing their horses. Topper was leading by at least a length, and they were still higher than the cabin and corrals. They saw a man come from the woods some distance back of the house. He was carrying an axe, and he was beyond the house, with it between himself and the outlaws. Suddenly a shot rang out. The man hesitated, then broke into a run for the house.

The three riders had covered a good mile and were closing down on the ranch, well scattered, when that shot sounded. At almost the same instant there was a piercing scream from a horse and a choked cry from a man. All were close enough to see a huge red stallion wheel on the man in the corral and rush for him. The outlaw turned, grabbed wildly for the top bar of the corral, and threw his leg up. The leg never got there, for the enraged stallion seized the man in his teeth and jerked back.

The outlaw fell—it was the Breed—then lunged to his feet. Before any of them could act, it was all over. The stallion rushed him, reared, and struck out. A flying hoof caught the Breed and struck him down, and instantly the horse went into a pitching, striking fury. The animal was fiendish, striking again and again at the silent, sprawled-out figure.

White of face, Hopalong turned away from the corral. Mesquite, tough as he was, was drawing back, looking sick. Then a man rushed from the house, belting on his guns. He slowed when he saw the three.

Sprawled in the open, outside the corral, was Slim. He had been shot through the body, but he was still alive.

"Only one good horse," he muttered. "When the Breed saw that, he just grabbed iron. I never had a chance."

The rancher was puzzled. "What's goin' on?" he said, his brows furrowed. "Why were they fighting over my horse?"

Hopalong motioned to the outlaws' sagging mounts. "Ran their own almost to death," he said quietly. "We were right behind 'em. A couple of rustlers. I guess the Breed aimed to have that horse for himself."

"He got him," Red said, "and though I hate to see any horse kill a man, that one had it comin'."

The rancher looked relieved. "I was afraid he was a friend of you boys," he said. "I was afraid there would be trouble. That stallion's a killer, all right. But he's the best stud around here. He don't bother me none," he added, "because I feed him and I always move slow around him. But he's afraid of a rope. Scared to death of one."

Hopalong was still kneeling by Slim. He had seen at once there was nothing that could be done. The man was dying. Slim's eyes lifted to Hopalong's.

"Gave you a run for your money," he said. "Wish I could have died in better company than that Breed. He wasn't . . .

he wasn't fit for no man. The Injuns wouldn't have him around; neither would the Mexicans. He was mean—awful . . . mean."

Slim lay quiet, breathing raggedly for several minutes, then started to speak. His lips formed the words, then failed; he was no longer living.

The rancher stared down at him, then looked up, his eyes going from one to the other of the three men. "Don't believe I know you," he said carefully. "Who might you be?"

Hopalong turned to him. "Hopalong Cassidy," he said, "and this is Red Connors, and Mesquite Jenkins. Those men were rustlers robbing the ranches around Tascotal."

The man grinned at Hopalong. "Heard of you," he admitted.

All through the remainder of the afternoon they rode on, keeping to the east and following a series of broken valleys and cuts that gave them a route through the north-and-south-running ranges of mountains. Toward the evening it grew cool, and darkness came suddenly. They made camp in a grove of fir clustered in a fold among the hills. At daylight they were again riding.

Hopalong pointed suddenly. "Something lying over there. Let's have a look."

Loping their horses through the grass, they drew up on the hillside where the grass thinned down among the rocks. What Hopalong had seen was a mule deer. It had been dead for some time.

Red swung down and turned the animal over. "Shot," he said. "Died sometime yesterday or the day before."

All knew who might have fired the shot, and knew there was every chance that Jack Bolt was in the vicinity. The rancher had known nothing of Bolt, nor of any cabin recently built. He had, several days past, while hunting far to the east, heard a rifle shot. He had believed it to be somebody riding through the country, or a prospector.

Since leaving him the three had cut old trails, but nothing that indicated any recent signs of travel. The dead deer was the first indication of life in the area that was anything but animal. Red looked speculatively at the deer. "What d'yuh think, Hoppy? Would he come far?"

"No more than a couple of miles with that wound."

"Then the best place to look," Mesquite suggested, "would be over that ridge?"

Hopalong nodded, studying it with no liking. "That's it," he agreed. He looked around at them. "And be careful. Bolt will probably shoot on sight. We'll scatter out to cross that ridge and look for trail sign." He indicated a towering, lightning-blasted pine on the crest of the ridge. "We'll meet at sundown right below that pine. If shooting starts, we all know what to do."

CHAPTER 24

Outlaw at Bay

When he was alone Hopalong got down and tightened his cinch. He had elected to follow the path of the deer. The hunter who had shot it might be miles from home, but he knew that there were many deer in this country and very few hunters, so it was unlikely that any hunter would have to go far to kill a deer, nor would he be likely to kill one far from home and so have to pack it back. In most of these mountain cabins a man could step out almost any morning and kill his deer within a matter of minutes.

"If I had to guess," he murmured, "I'd say within three miles of here. And it would be a good guess."

Water—shelter—fuel.

The first thing when he was over the rise would be to hunt a watercourse or possible spring.

It would be in good timber, and in a locality not easily seen from a distance.

There would be signs of woodcutting, without a doubt. Though probably there would be little cut within the immediate vicinity. The cabin would be in deep woods or in some fold of the hills. He mounted, spoke softly to Topper, and started up the slope. The trail of the deer was dim, but visible. It led upward at an angle toward the ridge.

The actual crest was heavily forested with fir, and between the rocks were splashes of squaw mat, but only a few of the brilliant blue flowers remained. Here and there was an immense sugar pine, giving way as he climbed higher to mountain hemlock and red fir. The deer had fallen and struggled erect twice on that slope, for he had been weakening fast here, and all sense of locality must have long since been gone. At both places the gravel and squaw mat were stained dark by lost blood.

Turning away from the trail, Hopalong bent his head and rode into a thick, dark section of fir. Here he sat right atop the ridge and could see over a wide stretch of country, but he could see no smoke or suggestion of it; all he could see were treetops. The valley beyond the mountain was high but heavily forested. Returning to the deer trail, Hopalong followed it over the ridge.

Within a few minutes he had found the nest where the deer had bedded down. Evidently it had used this place a great deal, and apparently the hunter had either stumbled upon it or had deliberately hunted it down. After a careful study of the country brought no reward, Hopalong swung out from the deer's nest until he was a good fifty feet away from it and then began a slow, watchful circle of the spot. Almost sixty yards from the nest he came upon the trail. A man in high-heeled boots had stood here and had fired twice. He found both shells among the needles. They were from a Winchester .44–40.

He turned abruptly and swung into the leather, turning the white gelding down the slope into the trees. For a short distance he followed the trail, then halted abruptly. Clear and sharp against the air he heard the sound of an axe. Rising in the stirrups he looked through the trees and for the first time saw the cabin.

Set back in a notch among the hills, it was screened by trees, and he could see behind it the line of a watercourse he had noticed several minutes before. As he watched, a man stopped chopping and gathered an armful of wood, walking toward the house. Even from this distance he could see it was Grat. The man turned at the step and took a last look around, then went inside.

Hopalong did not hesitate. He could wait until sundown and then return with the others, but he decided against it. Mesquite was impetuous, and if he found the cabin he would barge right in. It would be better to go ahead. There was just a chance he might take them both alive, although even as the thought passed through his mind he knew the chances were slight.

He rode the horse downhill for three hundred yards, then concealed him among the trees and brush in a little hollow near a leaning slab of rock. Leaving his Winchester behind, he started down the slope through the trees.

The cabin was backed against the mountain and could be approached from only one direction—straight in front. To the left of the avenue before him were the corrals; to the right, flowing between the house and himself, was the stream. It was only a few inches deep, but about four or five feet wide.

It was growing late. The afternoon sun was already down over the mountain in the west. Long shadows were gathering, although the sky overhead was still bright and the few scattered clouds were faintly pink. The storm that had been threatening for the last two days was piling up clouds again, and in the distance there was thunder.

There was only one way to approach the cabin, and Hopalong hesitated, disliking the look of the situation. Suddenly Bolt came from the house and walked with quick, nervous strides down toward the horses. He wore two guns and had a third thrust in his waistband. As he walked, his eyes probed restlessly at the woods and the ridges.

Abruptly, when not over forty yards from Hopalong, he stopped. Nervously he looked around. Hopalong's intent gaze might have warned him, or he believed he had heard something. He looked around, and as his eyes went past the place where Hopalong waited, Hopalong stepped into the open. Instantly the eyes swung back to him, and the two men faced each other across the clearing.

"Cassidy?" Bolt asked. "Is that you?"

Hopalong took a step toward the gunman. "It's me, all right. Expect me?"

Bolt watched him, his eyes intent. "Sort of. I hoped you'd come. You're the one who caused all this for me! You butted in where you had no business. If you'd stayed out, why, I'd have my ranch now and be in California enjoying it."

"And some good honest people would have lost most of their cattle," Hopalong said. "I think this way is better."

"You won't think it long." Bolt was almost pleasant. Hopalong started toward him, walking slowly, narrowing the distance.

The gunman's face was haggard, and his eyes seemed wild. His face was unshaven and his clothes untidy. He seemed to have become ragged of nerve and irritable to an extent he had never been before. He was facing Hopalong, but suddenly he turned his right side toward him, his hand suspended over his gun. "Looking for it, Cassidy? I'm not Pod Griffin, you know."

Hopalong said nothing, bearing suddenly to the left. This maneuver confused Bolt, as he could not see the sense in it. Actually, its sole purpose was to confuse the gunman and to make him turn; also to get out of the line of a possible shot from the cabin door. Suddenly, Hopalong stopped. He was now within thirty yards of the outlaw, and Bolt was glaring at him, wide-eyed with hate. "If I had been sure you wouldn't go back to bother those people," Hopalong said, "I'd not have come after you."

Bolt chuckled, and the sound was dry. Somewhere in the distance thunder rumbled. "You can just bet I was going back! I was going back after the rest of their cattle and to burn them out! Sim will catch up to me—"

"Sim's dead."

"There's his brothers, the Breed, Slim—"

"Slim was killed by the Breed in a fight over a horse. The horse killed the Breed. As for the Aragons, Manuel is badly wounded and Pete in jail."

Jack Bolt stared at him. "So? There are others." He looked more closely at Hopalong. "You killed Sim Aragon?"

Hopalong nodded.

Jack Bolt shrugged, and then as his shoulders lifted in the shrug both hands grabbed gun butts. His face twisted in a wolfish snarl and the guns leaped from the leather. Hopalong ran two quick steps, stopped, and his guns bucked as his heels braced. Bolt's body jerked, he half-turned, then swung a gun on Hopalong and fired!

Hopalong felt the tug at his shirt sleeve and he shot again and again. Each bullet knocked Bolt back a step as it struck, and he stood swaying at the end, his eyes still ugly with hatred.

"You're fast, Cassidy!" he said. "But—" His voice ended

and his mouth opened, gasping for words. Then he was dropping, falling face downward into the dirt.

Thunder rumbled again and there were a few spattering drops of rain. Hopalong turned his eyes toward the cabin. Grat stood on the steps, his hands empty. For a long minute their eyes held over the distance between them.

"I ain't fightin', Cassidy. I've had enough. If you won't let them lynch me, I'll come along willin'."

"All right," Hopalong replied. "I'll make sure you get a fair trial."

Just then Mesquite Jenkins rode into the clearing, leading Topper. A moment behind him was Red Connors. Both men looked at Bolt, then at Hopalong. "You hurt?" Mesquite asked.

"No." Cassidy looked down at Bolt, his face strangely white in the fading light. "Bring him up to the barn, will you, Red? It's going to rain."

Grat was standing at the table with a steaming coffeepot when they came in. He had put four plates on the table. "Chuck's ready," he said. "Set and eat."

All three looked at him a moment, then nodded. Without further hesitation they sat down, and he loaded their plates with food. "My guns and ammunition are on the bunk," he said. He filled Red's cup, then looked down at him. "We gave you a bad time in the hills, Red. I reckon I'm sorry about that. You were mighty game."

Red shrugged. "That's past. You make a good cup of coffee."

Hopalong looked from one to the other, and faint lines appeared around his eyes. These were his kind of men. Winning or losing, they made no great fuss about it.

Thunder rolled and there was a swift, rushing spatter of

raindrops. From where he sat he could see through the open door and smell the odor of rain on long-dry dust.

The storm might last for several days. He leaned back and stretched his legs under the table. The coffee was strong, black, and hot.

A NOTE OF EXPLANATION AND THANKS

For those of you who have not read *The Rustlers of West Fork* and its Afterword, here is a brief history of my father's involvement with Hopalong Cassidy stories:

In the early 1950s, actor William Boyd took his version of the Cassidy character from the big screen to television. His earlier movies and Clarence Mulford's Hopalong books had been very popular, and so Doubleday, Mulford's publisher, became interested in marketing some new Hoppy novels. Mulford, who had been retired since 1941, did not want to continue the job, and so he turned the task over to a young (actually not that young; Dad was forty-two) writer of pulp magazine westerns . . . Louis L'Amour.

The publisher chose the pen name Tex Burns for him, and in 1950 and '51 he wrote his four Hopalong Cassidy books. They were published as the feature stories in the short-lived periodical *Hopalong Cassidy's Western Magazine* and in hardcover by Doubleday. Due to a disagreement with the publisher over which interpretation of the Hopalong character to use (Dad wanted to use Mulford's original Hoppy, a red-haired, hard-drinking, foul-mouthed, and rather bellicose cowhand instead of Doubleday's preference for the slick, heroic portrayal that Boyd adopted for his films), my father refused to admit that he had ever written those last four Hopalongs. Starting with *The Rustlers of West Fork*, this is the first time they have been published with his name on them. For a more in-depth version of the story of how Louis L'Amour came to write and then deny that he had written the Cassidy stories, you can take a look at the Afterword in *Rustlers*.

I again offer my thanks to David R. Hastings II and Peter G.

Hastings, trustees of the Clarence E. Mulford Trust. Also to the late C. E. Mulford himself for creating the classic character of Hopalong Cassidy.

My best to you all,

Beau L'Amour
Los Angeles, California
November 1992

ABOUT LOUIS L'AMOUR

"I think of myself in the oral tradition—as a troubadour, a village tale-teller, the man in the shadows of the campfire. That's the way I'd like to be remembered—as a storyteller. A good storyteller."

It is doubtful that any author could be as at home in the world re-created in his novels as Louis Dearborn L'Amour. Not only could he physically fill the boots of the rugged characters he wrote about, but he literally "walked the land my characters walk." His personal experiences as well as his lifelong devotion to historical research combined to give Mr. L'Amour the unique knowledge and understanding of people, events, and the challenge of the American frontier that became the hallmarks of his popularity.

Of French-Irish descent, Mr. L'Amour could trace his own family in North America back to the early 1600s and follow their steady progression westward, "always on the frontier." As a boy growing up in Jamestown, North Dakota, he absorbed all he could about his family's frontier heritage, including the story of his great-grandfather who was scalped by Sioux warriors.

Spurred by an eager curiosity and desire to broaden his horizons, Mr. L'Amour left home at the age of fifteen and enjoyed a wide variety of jobs including seaman, lumberjack, elephant handler, skinner of dead cattle, assessment miner, and an officer in the tank destroyers during World War II. During his "yondering" days he also circled the world on a freighter, sailed a dhow on the Red Sea, was shipwrecked in the West Indies and stranded in the Mojave Desert. He won fifty-one of fifty-nine fights as a professional boxer and worked as a journalist and lecturer. He was a voracious reader and collector of rare books. His personal library contained 17,000 volumes.

Mr. L'Amour "wanted to write almost from the time I could talk." After developing a widespread following for his many frontier and adventure stories written for fiction magazines, Mr. L'Amour published his first full-length novel, *Hondo*, in the United States in 1953. Every one of his more than 100 books is in print; there are nearly 230 million copies of his books in print worldwide, making him one of the bestselling authors in modern literary history. His books have been translated into twenty languages, and more than forty-five of his novels and stories have been made into feature films and television movies.

His hardcover bestsellers include *The Lonesome Gods, The Walking Drum* (his twelfth-century historical novel), *Jubal Sackett, Last of the Breed,* and *The Haunted Mesa.* His memoir, *Education of a Wandering Man,* was a leading bestseller in 1989. Audio dramatizations and adaptations of many L'Amour stories are available on cassette tapes from Bantam Audio publishing.

The recipient of many great honors and awards, in 1983 Mr. L'Amour became the first novelist ever to be awarded the Congressional Gold Medal by the United States Congress in honor of his life's work. In 1984 he was also awarded the Medal of Freedom by President Reagan.

Louis L'Amour died on June 10, 1988. His wife, Kathy, and their two children, Beau and Angelique, carry the L'Amour tradition forward with new books written by the author during his lifetime to be published by Bantam well into the nineties—among them, an additional Hopalong Cassidy novel, *Trouble Shooter.*